That's Not Strategy

Where the future thrives in the choices of today

Michael Parsons

Dedication

To the Weiss family. Your love and support have given this nomad a place to call home. You've traveled the world with your boys in tow to wherever I've been making a life, opening your door, sharing your food, and welcoming me as one of your own. I've loved every moment shared in your lives.

Acknowledgment

To the guest speakers, professors, mentors, and school leaders who challenged my thinking, asked hard questions, and reminded me that theory only matters if it changes how we serve students, and especially to Janelle Simpkins, whose encouragement, knowledge, strategic mindset, and unwavering belief in me continually pushed me forward. Thank you for sharing your valuable time, your insights about this book and its importance, and for reminding me again and again why I needed to keep going.

About the Author

Michael Parsons is an international educator, strategist, and storyteller who has spent more than two decades helping schools find clarity in the chaos of change. From classrooms in the United States to leadership roles across Africa, Asia, and the Middle East, his work centers on one belief: strategy, not busyness, turns good intentions into lasting impact.

A former Director of Teaching and Learning and now Data and Assessment Coordinator, Michael is known for building data-informed, purpose-driven schools. He created the Bullseye Strategy Model to help educators move from scattered initiatives to coherent, values-based action.

He holds an MBA in Educational Leadership with an emphasis on Strategic Management and Organizational Behaviour. Michael is also a high-level coach, conference presenter, and certified personal trainer who believes clarity, discipline, and reflection drive both learning and leadership.

Table of Contents

Dear Reader

If you've picked up this book, you're probably someone who cares deeply about learning, whether you teach it, lead it, support it, or simply believe in its power to change lives. You are not looking for the next program, a new set of buzzwords, or a glossy plan that looks good in a slide deck. You are looking for coherence, for clarity, for a way to make choices that actually lead to creating lasting change for students.

I have spent my career learning that meaningful improvement begins with courage and focus. It requires us to slow down long enough to ask, *What truly matters here?* It challenges us to hold that focus when the easier path is to keep adding more. It asks us to say no to what sounds good but does not serve the goal. And most of all, meaningful improvement reminds us that strategy is not about control, it is about clarity.

Over the years, I have come to believe that strategy is an act of empathy as much as it is an act of logic. It is the bridge between intention and impact, between what we value and what we actually do. It gives teachers, leaders, and communities the confidence to act with purpose, and not just activity.

You will not find promises of doing more in the pages ahead. You will find a commitment to doing what matters with focus, honesty, and courage to hold the line when things get difficult. If that is what you are after, you are in the right place.

With respect and relentless curiosity,

Michael Parsons

Preface: We've Got It All Backwards

In schools, the phrase strategic planning gets used a lot. It sounds responsible. Thoughtful. Visionary.

But most of the time, it's simply just a list of tasks dressed up as strategy.

We gather feedback, hold workshops, write it all down, print a slick document, and call it a plan. Then we move on to the next initiative, the next PD cycle, the next school year. And we wonder why nothing really sticks.

It's not that people aren't working hard. They are. But we've mistaken planning for progress. We've come to believe that being busy means we're being strategic.

The truth is, strategy isn't a process. Most don't realize it's a theory.

It's a belief about what will help us win, based on who we are developing, where we are now, and what we think will make the biggest difference. That belief needs to be clear, bold, and tested. Most importantly, it needs to guide the choices we make every day.

And that's where things usually fall apart.

Because a real strategy isn't comfortable, it means deciding what not to do. It means focusing on fewer things and doing them better. It means living with the risk that your theory might be wrong.

This book started with a sense of frustration. I kept seeing school's drift. Not because people didn't care, but because they didn't know where they were going. I kept hearing phrases like "this aligns with our strategic plan" when no one could actually say what success would look like. We were making decisions without a strategy. We were calling it a strategy because it sounded better than "we're figuring it out as we go."

That's Not Strategy is my response to that.

It's not a playbook. It's not a shortcut. It's a way to think differently about the work we do in schools.

I wrote it for leaders who want clarity, not just compliance. For teachers who want to understand how their work connects to something bigger. And for communities that deserve more than buzzwords and patchwork fixes.

Real strategy starts with five questions:

- Who are we really here for?
- Where are we now?
- Why does this work matter?
- How will we know if it's working?
- What will we commit to doing on purpose?

If you're tired of planning cycles that don't change anything, and ready to build something that actually moves a school forward, you're in the right place. Let's get to work.

Introduction: That's Not Strategy

Where the future thrives in the choices of today

Meet Carolyn.

It's 2026. She's just entered Grade 2. She will graduate in 2036, stepping into a future we can't fully imagine. The industries will be different. The tools will be unrecognizable. Artificial intelligence won't be a novelty, but her co-pilot. She will face problems we haven't yet named and navigate challenges we haven't even begun to understand.

But one thing will be true. Carolyn's future will be shaped by the choices schools make today.

Now imagine a school built for that future.

Not built on programs.

Not built on Canva-worthy initiative maps or a color-coded improvement plan.

Instead, it's built on strategy.

A school that knows who it's trying to develop.

Understands where it is now.

And makes deliberate, measurable choices about how to move forward.

This is Carolyn's school.

It's fictional, but it doesn't have to be.

Let's be honest. If you've worked in schools long enough, you've probably sat through a meeting that goes something like this:

A new initiative is unveiled with a polished slide deck, a flurry of acronyms, and the classic assurance:

"This aligns with our strategic priorities."

There are nods around the table. There may even be a few hopeful smiles.

Then I ask the question that tends to halt the momentum: "How will we know if it worked?"

The room goes quiet.

Because the truth is, no one really knows. We know it feels like a good idea. We know it sounds strategic. But when it comes to identifying a measurable outcome or tracking real impact, that's where things tend to fall apart.

Schools aren't short on ideas.

What we're short on is strategy.

We confuse planning with strategy. We equate being busy with having purpose. We create initiatives in response to problems, but not always in response to a clear, measurable goal. And once we've invested time and energy, we're reluctant to ask whether any of it actually worked.

It's not that educators don't care, but quite the opposite. Most school leaders and teachers I've worked with are deeply committed to doing what's best for students. But that commitment often gets tangled in too many initiatives, unclear objectives, and a lack of feedback loops.

In education, strategy is too often confused with vision statements, planning templates, or long lists of tasks on a school accreditation document. People believe they are being strategic when they are, in fact, just being busy. And once that belief sets in, they stop questioning it.

We get caught in what I call a perpetual cycle of planning. Everything looks active, but not much is actually moving forward.

It's a textbook example of the Dunning-Kruger effect: the less someone understands a complex concept, the more confident they are in their ability to master it. Strategy is one of those concepts. It's misused so often in schools that many don't realize they're missing it entirely.

"A wealth of information creates a poverty of attention."
– Herbert Simon

And a flood of initiatives creates a poverty of focus.

From Experience

I've spent over two decades in education, teaching, leading, coaching, designing systems, and building cultures of data-informed practice. My work has taken me across six countries and every major division in K–12 education.

Along the way, I pursued an MBA in Educational Leadership, not to manage schools more efficiently, but to understand how organizations function at a deeper level. I wanted to explore how mission, behavior, systems, and decision-making connect and why, so often, they don't.

What I've learned over time is simple but powerful.

Strategy is not a plan.

Strategy is a theory.

A bet about how you'll succeed, grounded in values and tested by evidence.

It's a set of deliberate choices:

- Where you play: what you will and won't focus on
- How you win: how you'll create value in ways that truly matter
- What you need: the systems and people that make it real

It says:

"This is what we believe will work. This is how we'll act on it. And this is how we'll know if we're wrong."

In the business world, strategy is often described as a set of choices: where to play, how to win, and what it takes to deliver. While the context is different, the core logic applies in schools as well.

But in education, the real competition isn't against other schools.

It is between what education is today and what it needs to become.

Today, schools face a tension between satisfying the expectations of parents, rooted in the schools of their past, and building a system that prepares students like Carolyn for the world ahead. It is a world we cannot fully predict, but we know it will demand far more than grades and compliance.

A Future You Cannot Yet See

Carolyn will need to think critically, act ethically, adapt quickly, and learn continuously.

If our current structures, plans, and initiatives aren't preparing her for that world, what are they doing?

That's why this book exists. To ask the harder question:

If we're not being intentional about the future we're building, then what exactly are we doing?

Strategy isn't about reacting to the past.

It's about designing the future on purpose.

Can I Ask a Question?

If you've ever worked with me, you've heard this phrase more than once:

"I've got a question for you."

My friend Andrew, affectionately known as Big Bear, would laugh whenever he heard me say it.

But that's where strategy starts. It starts with the right questions.

The ones that expose assumptions, clarify thinking, and force us to define what we're actually trying to accomplish.

What Strategy Looks Like in Schools

Let's bring it into focus.

Strategy in schools is a set of intentional leadership decisions:

- **Where you focus**: The student needs, programs, and priorities you will commit to, and just as importantly, those you will not.

- **How you deliver impact:** how your school will design learning experiences that prepare students for a future filled with complexity, uncertainty, and opportunity that will not just meet the standards of today but shape the world of tomorrow.

- **What you require to succeed:** the staff, structures, and systems needed to make that vision a reality in every classroom.

If our strategy is only designed to satisfy the present, we are failing the future.

The job of leadership is to maintain that tension.

To make choices today that serve the world our students will inherit tomorrow.

That is what real strategy demands.

Because when we don't do this, when there is no clear strategy, school's default to drift.

The slow, quiet erosion of focus where everyone is busy, but no one is sure why.

In that space, even the most dedicated educators start making decisions based not on what matters most, but on what is immediately in front of them.

They don't do it out of malice, but from a lack of shared direction.

A Lesson from Baseball

If you haven't watched Moneyball, put it on your list. Yes, it's about baseball, but it's also about strategy in action.

The Oakland A's didn't have the money to compete with powerhouse teams, so they changed the game. They stopped focusing on what everyone else said mattered and zeroed in on what actually led to wins: getting on base.

They didn't just play differently. Instead, they redefined the playing field.

Now, that's strategy. A clear, data-informed theory of success, executed with discipline, even when everyone else thinks you've lost your mind.

What This Book Offers

This book is written for school leaders, curriculum coordinators, teacher-leaders, board members, and anyone serious about aligning what a school says it values with what it actually achieves.

If you've ever felt that your school is doing a lot but achieving too little, this book is for you.

Inside, you'll find:

- A clear, practical definition of strategy, and how it differs from planning
- The Bullseye Strategy Framework, helping you connect values, goals, and actions
- Strategic case studies and examples in:
  - Approaches to Learning (ATL): fostering strategic, reflective, self-directed learners
  - SEL: building empathy, resilience, and integrity
  - Reading: developing engaged, critical, and proficient readers

- o   Math: growing rational, fluent, and confident problem-solvers
- Organizational strategy guides:
  - o   Wellness and Professionalism
- Tools to define success, track progress, and avoid the illusion of improvement

This isn't a book about theory just for the sake of theory. It's a blueprint for turning ideas into impact, built from years of working alongside educators who were ready to think differently.

If your school is serious about transforming culture, aligning actions with values, and building a system that doesn't just do more, but does what matters, then this is your starting point.

Because in a world where every school has a mission but few have a strategy, it's time to ask:

Are we doing what works, or just doing what we've always done?

"The essence of strategy is choosing what not to do."

– Michael Porter

Strategic Self-Check: How Strategic Is Your School?

Before diving deeper, take a moment to reflect.

Think about your school's most recent initiative or major program shift.

- Was it launched in response to a clearly defined, strategic objective?
- Did you have measurable outcomes in place before starting?
- Can you trace a line from that initiative to your school's long-term values and goals?

If you're unsure or answered "no" to any of the above, you're not alone. Most schools confuse action with impact and mistake planning for strategy.

Now, assess your school's current strategic standing. Rate each statement from 1 (Not at All) to 5 (Fully True):

1. We have a clearly articulated strategic vision that guides all major decisions

2. Our initiatives are designed in response to specific, measurable desired impacts

3. We use defined KPIs or success metrics to track and adjust our initiatives

4. School leaders can explain how current programs directly support long-term goals

5. We say "no" to initiatives that don't align with our strategy, even if they're popular or exciting

Scoring Key:

5–10 | Drifting. You're active but unanchored. This book will help you find direction

11–17 | Planning-Driven. You're organized, but the impact isn't intentional. The strategy is waiting to be unlocked

18–23 | Emerging Strategist. You're making moves that matter. This book will sharpen your edge

24–25 | Strategy Mastery. You're on target. Use this book to refine, scale, and mentor others

Let's get to work.

For Carolyn.

For every student who deserves a school built on strategy, not slogans.

Chapter 1: What's Not Strategy

Let's start with a gut check.

If someone asked your leadership team to explain your school's strategy, on one page, in plain language, could they do it?

Could your teachers connect today's PD session or new initiative to a long-term theory of impact?

Could your students articulate the kind of learner they're being shaped to become, not just what they're doing, but who they're becoming?

If the answer is no, that's not a failure of intelligence or passion. It's a failure of clarity. It's not that we lack effort; we often lack a shared anchor. And that's not a strategy.

That's drift.

We're not drifting because we don't care. We're drifting because we haven't agreed on what matters most.

As a die-hard Toronto Blue Jays fan, I've long known the pain of watching a bad call unfold in slow motion. It's almost a tradition. Buck Martinez, the Jays' play-by-play announcer, has a knack for saying something right before disaster strikes: "This batter has never hit a homerun off this Jays starter..." You already know what's about to happen. We turned it into a drinking game and took a chug, broke the jinx, and gave the Jays a chance!

I've brought the same game to staff meetings. Except now it's about the word "strategy." I keep a tally chart:

+1 for every time it's used correctly,

−1 for every time it's misused, misapplied, or thrown around like seasoning on a dish that never needed it.

Over the last year, I've tracked my little experiment. The score? −78. Each minus point is more than a misuse of language; it's a unit of credibility lost, a measure of time and energy misdirected. It's a lot of chugs and it made me think, "That's Not Strategy!'

Strategy isn't just a buzzword to make a meeting feel important. It's a disciplined, coherent set of choices. And yet, we hear it casually attached to everything from a way to divide fractions to new PD sessions. The result? We start to lose faith in the idea of strategy altogether, and more worryingly, we lose clarity on what actually matters.

What makes it more troubling is that many of these misuses are well-intentioned. Educators want to improve, leaders want to inspire, and schools want to move forward. But the misuse of the word strategy reflects a deeper issue: we're trying to shortcut the hard work of prioritizing, sequencing, and evaluating.

If everything is called strategy, then nothing is. We end up in meetings where people nod enthusiastically about "strategic planning" without agreeing on what success looks like. Initiatives are rolled out with no baselines, no measurable goals, and no accountability, just belief and hope. And in education, belief is a powerful force, but belief without evidence isn't a strategy. It's hope.

So, when Buck Martinez sets up a disaster with a well-meaning observation, we brace ourselves. And when school leaders toss around "strategy" without defining what it actually means, maybe we should do the same, not because we're cynical, but because we care enough to want it done right.

Strategy isn't a slogan. It's not a plan you roll out once a year and forget by February. It's not just a list of great ideas. It's also not something to be built on the fly. Some of the most exciting initiatives in education have fizzled, not because they weren't good, but because they weren't grounded in a clear, cohesive strategy. This chapter is a gentle but honest check-up for school leaders: a chance to notice where we may be mistaking motion for progress.

Overconfidence without the underlying know-how

This misuse of "strategy" isn't about bad intentions; it's often about overconfidence without the underlying know-how. The Dunning-Kruger effect is a psychological quirk where people with less expertise sometimes overestimate their abilities. In schools, this often appears when well-meaning leaders, promoted for their instructional or relational strengths, are tasked with leading strategic initiatives without having received formal training in strategy itself.

The truth is that most educational leadership programs focus on supervision, operations, and curriculum, not strategic theory, decision-making frameworks, or organizational positioning. As a result, leaders often enter these roles with good intentions but little preparation for the choices strategy requires. And in the absence of strategic clarity, schools fall into cycles of doing more, not better.

Some international schools are beginning to recognize this gap. New roles like Chief Strategy Officer or Director of Strategy are emerging, signaling that perhaps strategy deserves its own chair at the leadership table. But even without new titles, the question remains: Should school leaders be trained in business acumen and strategic thinking? Leaders are expected to lead multi-million-dollar organizations, accountable to thousands of students, families, and staff. Shouldn't leaders at least learn the fundamentals of how to choose, prioritize, and win?

I've asked, "Why are we doing this?" more times than I can count. Too often, the answer is vague or defensive. For example, we once launched data retreats and data literacy workshops, promising in theory! But we skipped the first step: setting clear values. Without knowing what we were trying to accomplish, the work quickly became procedural. We checked boxes, held the sessions, and had no idea if they were making a difference.

As Mark Twain so perfectly put it, *"Data is like garbage. You'd better know what you are going to do with it before you collect it."* And yet, here we are, collecting with gusto and no disposal plan.

And then there's what I like to call the 'initiative shuffle.' Many schools experience it: over the course of a few years, multiple programs are introduced, perhaps around SEL, literacy, well-being, or instructional frameworks. Each one is thoughtfully chosen, often backed by research, and launched with energy and good intentions. But too often, they aren't tied to a specific outcome. There's no baseline. No clear success criteria. No plan for follow-up. Just a hopeful rollout and a quiet fade. When staff ask why something new is being introduced again, the answers are vague at best, and sometimes missing altogether.

The core issue here isn't the quality of the initiatives, it's the absence of strategic discipline behind them. If we were a business, we'd expect a return on investment. We'd define success before spending money. We'd check to see if what we did worked, and if not, we'd tweak or stop. Schools should be no different. Schools need to define success before spending the investment of teachers' time and energy into implementing initiatives.

Strategy does not mean playing it safe; it means playing to win. And yet, too often we confuse motion with progress. In the next section, I will unpack the blind spots that cause schools to drift, common failures that reassure us we are being "strategic," while quietly pulling us off course.

Common Blind spots That Masquerade as Strategy

Schools rarely stumble because of bad intentions. More often, they drift because leaders and teachers confuse activity with progress, or planning with strategy. These blind spots are subtle, but they slowly erode clarity and drain momentum.

Organizational Drift

Schools don't usually drift off course because of bad intentions. They drift because it's easy to confuse "doing a lot" with "doing what matters." I call this organizational drift, the kind that keeps everyone busy, but not necessarily effective.

Take Adaptive Schools (equips educators with the knowledge, skills, and strategies to enhance collaboration, build collective efficacy, and adapt to change. Its focus is on improving group dynamics, dialogue, and decision-making processes within schools, thereby strengthening the capacity of teams and organizations to work effectively toward shared goals.) for instance. Wonderful program. There had been little discussion with staff beforehand on what issues were being faced in terms of meeting structures, team dynamics, etc. No one knew why we were being offered the training in the first place. There certainly weren't non-negotiables to make leaders accountable for using any of this training once they had earned their shiny new certification. But we brought in an engaging facilitator for two weekends. People were fired up. Norms of collaboration made it into meeting agendas. And then… crickets.

No follow-up. No clarity on the goal. No data collection. A year later, you could barely find a trace of it. But we brought it back anyway, for another cohort. And guess what? Same pattern. Same result. Nobody really knew what problem it was supposed to solve.

Here's the thing: good programs can fall flat when they're dropped into unstrategic systems. Even the best tools need a structure to hold them. Without purpose, without follow-through, even the flashiest initiatives fade away.

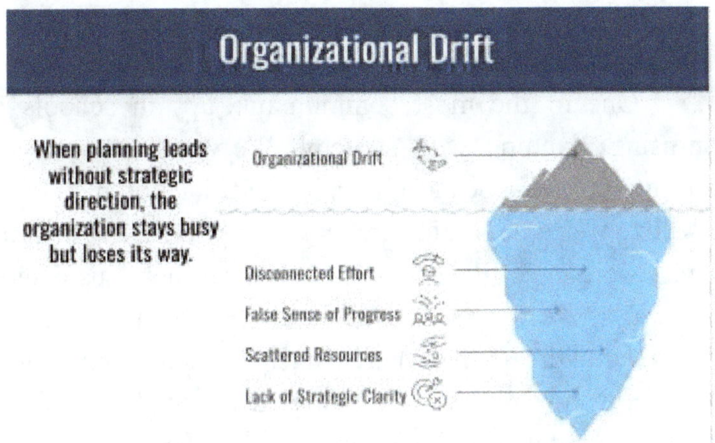

Figure 1: Organizational drift happens when schools confuse activity with impact. Without clarity, purpose, and follow-through, even strong programs fade, leaving disconnected efforts, scattered resources, and a false sense of progress beneath the surface.

Perpetual Planning and Vague Goals

Schools love to plan; we're champions of the detailed timeline and the color-coded chart. But without a clear purpose behind them, those plans can start to feel like theatre. We confuse agreement with alignment. Activity with intention. In meetings, I hear:

"I believe it was for…"
"It should be happening…"
"I assumed…"

As Albert Einstein famously said, *"Assumptions are made and most assumptions are wrong."* And yet, we base a surprising number of decisions on them.

That's not strategy, it's guesswork.

One of the most common mix-ups in schools is confusing planning with strategy. We've all been there, working through a beautifully color-coded action plan, only to realize we're not quite sure *why* we're doing it. Planning helps us organize time and tasks. Strategy helps us decide which tasks are worth doing in the first place. They're both essential, but they're not interchangeable. Think of planning as the GPS and strategy as choosing the destination. Without both, we might just be driving in circles, with very organized luggage.

And then there's the phrase we all love to hate: "We're flying the plane while building it." It's meant to sound daring. But in practice? It often feels like turbulence. Constant change without direction doesn't energize people; it exhausts them. When strategy is improvised, implementation becomes survival.

A solid strategy means making choices. It means knowing when to say no, so you can focus on what will truly move the needle. When schools skip this step, initiatives pile up, momentum fizzles, and people stop believing that anything will really stick.

As Sun Tzu wisely warned, *"Strategy without tactics is the slowest route to victory. Tactics without strategy is the noise before defeat."* And far too often, what schools call "strategic planning" ends up sounding like a drum circle of disconnected noise.

Initiative Overload

Every year, something new. New PD focus. New acronym. New platform. Sound familiar? When we layer initiative on top of initiative without letting go of what came before, or circling back to check effectiveness, we end up with what many staff experience as "initiative fatigue."

It's not just tiring, it's disheartening. Teachers disengage not because they don't care, but because they've learned the cycle. This year's priority will be next year's forgotten pilot. And we wonder why buy-in is hard to get.

Imagine a company spending thousands launching a new product without knowing its purpose, audience, or success metrics. It wouldn't last. But in schools, we tend to operate on passion and justify things with "we're different" or "every student matters."

Everything can't be a priority. That's not focus, that's not strategy.

Make Bold Coherent Choices

Roger Martin, strategist, author, and champion of clarity, reminds us that strategy isn't about certainty or control. It's about making bold, coherent choices in the face of uncertainty. It's not a menu of activities; it's a theory about how to win.

He argues that most strategic plans are simply collections of initiatives masquerading as strategy. Any logic or intent does not tie them together. They feel safe because they don't really commit to anything. But in Martin's words, *"If you're not making choices, you're not doing strategy."* The real test is this: can you explain your school's strategy on one page, without jargon? Can your team describe it the same way?

If not, don't worry, you're in good company. Most schools don't have a strategy problem. They have a clarity problem.

Vignettes from the Field

These are not rare stories. They're the everyday realities of schools that care deeply about improvement but find themselves drifting because of blind spots. As you read them, see if you can identify the patterns: the overconfidence without know-how, the initiative shuffle, the planning theatre, or the quiet pull of organizational drift.

Vignette 1: The Disappearing PD

One school launched a professional development initiative around visible learning. The slides were glossy, the kickoff was exciting, and for a short while, teachers even adjusted classroom practice. But no one could explain why visible learning had been chosen, or what problem it was meant to solve. There were no metrics, no follow-up, and no accountability. By the following year, it had quietly disappeared.

In another case, a school introduced curriculum standards but let each department select its own. Four years later, there was no consistency, no training, and no evidence that the standards had shaped teaching or assessment. Ask leadership why they were adopted, and you'd hear conflicting answers.

This is a textbook case of the **initiative shuffle**: programs chosen without a clear baseline, goal, or accountability structure. Roger Martin would say this is what happens when planning masquerades as strategy. You get movement without meaning. And yes, you can see the organizational drift here: people were busy, but not moving in the same direction.

Vignette 2: The Belief in Hope

An international school invested heavily in a well-being program. Training, curriculum, resources, the works. When asked what it was meant to achieve, the answer was vague: "We believe it will help with culture." Belief is powerful, but belief without evidence isn't a strategy. There was no data to support the claim, no baseline, no measurable goal. Two years later, the program was still running, but no one could say if it had made any difference.

Elsewhere, a school hosted data retreats twice a year. Teachers gathered to "look at trends," but without clear values, targets, or follow-up. There was no baseline, no end-of-year reflection, and no link to any larger strategy. The events became symbolic rituals rather than meaningful levers for change. Trust in the process eroded.

Here you see both **overconfidence without know-how** and the pull of **organizational drift**. Leaders assumed that because data retreats or well-being programs are inherently "good," they must be strategic. But as Roger Martin reminds us, strategy requires a theory of how these choices will actually create advantage. Without that theory, schools fall back on hope.

Final Thoughts

Reflective Prompt: Is Your School Strategic?

Strategy requires more than enthusiasm. It demands clarity, consistency, and courage. We need to be able to name the patterns we fall into, such as drift, overload, or misplaced confidence, so that we can address them. Strategy is not about sounding smart. It is about choosing smart.

This chapter is not here to scold. It is here to help. Think of it as a mirror we hold up to our systems, asking: Are we being thoughtful, or just busy?

During my time as Director of Teaching and Learning, especially in the turbulence of COVID-19, I came to see strategy in a new light. That season demanded rapid decisions under pressure. If I could go back, I would have started with staff wellness. In the end, a healthy team is a high-performing team. That is the strategy I wish I had led with.

I also know now that improvement, no matter how welcome, cannot automatically be counted as success. Growth without intention might be luck or circumstance. Strategy ensures that progress is not accidental. It makes sure we are not just getting better, but getting better on purpose.

In the next chapter, we'll stop circling what strategy isn't, and start building a shared understanding of what it truly is.

Before you turn the page, take a moment to consider:

- What were the last three initiatives your school introduced?
- What problem were they meant to solve?
- Was success clearly defined in advance?
- Was baseline data collected?
- Is there a plan to monitor and measure impact?
- Have any been sustained beyond one academic year?

If these questions feel tough to answer, you're not alone. But that's why they matter. Without answers, we're likely reacting, not strategizing. This isn't an indictment. It's an invitation to rethink how we lead, how we choose, and how we move forward together.

Chapter 2: What Is Strategy?

Brad Benson and I broke baseball.

Or at least that's how we like to tell it. Years before Major League teams began using analytics to shift defenses based on batter tendencies, we were testing those same theories, with a high school girls' softball team in Beijing.

In 2013, coaching the WAB girls' varsity softball team, we tracked every at-bat in our tournament. We gathered real data, game by game. And a pattern emerged: over 80% of balls in play were hit up the middle or to the left side of the diamond.

We weren't the most talented team in the tournament, but we were observant, motivated, and willing to try something new. We had a theory: if we could position our best fielders where the ball was *most likely* to go, we could "steal" outs, lower the opponent's runs, and keep games close. We figured we could give up five runs a game and still be competitive. So, we redesigned how we played defense.

It all started with three players: **Jojo**, **Estella**, and **Tia**. They were our best fielders, quick, smart, and fearless. Jojo locked down third base with fast hands and a rocket arm. Estella held shortstop with fluid movement and the kind of instincts you can't coach; she'd anticipate a play before the ball was hit. And Tia? Tia *wanted* the ball. She anchored first base with a calm intensity, a soft glove, and absolute fearlessness. Her confidence steadied the infield. She once told us, "Put me where the ball is hit most, I want to be in it."

We realized that if 80% of balls were going to the left and middle of the field, we needed Jojo, Estella, and Tia right in the line of fire. But we also needed Tia to *stay* at first; she saved runs and settled nerves. So, we got creative.

At the start of each inning, we lined up traditionally. But as soon as a runner reached first and the batter was right-handed (which was most of the time), we shifted. We moved Tia behind second base, reinforcing the middle. We left first base open.

Yes, really. Wide open.

We gave up the chance of a double play, rare anyway, and played for one out at a time. Our second baseman dropped into shallow right to grab bloops from batters trying to go to the opposite field. Our outfield was stacked from right-center to the left-field line. Every move had a reason. Based on the data, we were betting on probability and execution.

Other coaches thought we were out of our minds. At the post-game dinner, our shift was the talk of the room. Our girls didn't debate this strategy, but the other coaches did. The girls believed in it. Because we'd made the strategy *clear*, and they could see it *working*. They weren't just playing the game; they were *executing a theory*. They saw the results. They *owned* the shift. Each time they made a play from the new formation, we celebrated it: "You just stole an out." They tracked those moments. It became part of the culture. They weren't just reacting to the game; they were executing a strategy they understood.

We rode that approach to our first-ever finals appearance. We lost in the last inning, 7–6. But the pride was palpable. These girls had gone from winning their first game as a team the year before to tournament finalists. Not just because they worked hard, but because they followed a strategy they believed in. Clearly, our success was so groundbreaking that it convinced Major League Baseball teams to adopt our theory a few years later. ;-)

That's what strategy is.

Strategy Is a Theory

Too often, people assume strategy is about slogans or operational flowcharts. It is not. Strategy is a theory of success.

It says: Given who we are and where we are, here is what we believe will give us the best chance to achieve our goals.

Strategy is not a checklist. It is a hypothesis, a belief grounded in values, context, and evidence about how we can influence the outcomes that matter. It is a deliberate set of choices that shape how we use time, energy, people, and resources.

Michael Porter captured it well: *"Strategy 101 is about choices. You can't be all things to all people."*

That quote cuts especially deep in education, where schools are constantly pulled in competing directions. We want to be rigorous and creative, standardized and personalized, inquiry-based and results-driven. In trying to be everything, we risk becoming nothing in particular.

Without a strategy, schools default to busyness instead of effectiveness. Every new initiative gets added to the pile, under the false belief that more activity will mean more progress. In reality, it usually produces fragmentation and fatigue.

A good strategy forces a school to choose. It demands clarity about trade-offs, alignment around what matters most, and belief in a theory of action coherent enough to guide decisions even if it is not yet proven.

Richard Rumelt explains: *"A good strategy honestly acknowledges the challenges being faced and provides an approach to overcoming them. Bad strategy is long on goals and short on insight. It treats challenges as if they will dissolve by merely stating ambitions."*

Education is often guilty of this. We set ambitious goals, like "increase student agency" or "foster global citizens," but fail to define the coherent actions that would make them real. Strategy is the bridge between ambition and action.

Done well, strategy is not about doing more. It is about doing what matters, with focus and purpose, and with enough clarity to follow through. Done poorly, the opposite happens. Schools push forward with more initiatives, which create less progress, more fragmentation, and deeper fatigue. The unintended result is often toxic cultures, growing hopelessness, and staff exhaustion, all of which ultimately fall hardest on students.

Start with WHO and WHERE

A strong strategy starts with clarity about two things:

- **WHO** you are, your values, your beliefs about learning, and the non-negotiables that define your identity.
- **WHERE** you are, your current performance, your strengths, your gaps, your context.

The softball team knew both.

WHO we were: a group of girls who knew they needed to do something bold to be in a position to win.

WHERE we were: a team coming off years of losses, needing belief and traction.

From that clarity, the strategy emerged.

Softball Strategy: analyze data from other teams' games, identify their hitting patterns, and place our best fielders in the most likely positions where the ball is most likely to be hit.

It was simple, but it was a coherent theory: if we positioned ourselves based on evidence rather than habit, we would give ourselves the best chance to win.

In schools, the same logic applies. If you say you value student agency, how does your strategy reflect that in practice? If you claim to be data-informed, where are you actually using data to guide decisions, not just to monitor performance?

Strategy connects the gap between aspiration and action. But it can only do that if you first define who you are and where you are starting from.

Strategy vs. Planning

This confusion is common: planning is *not* strategy.

Planning asks: *How will we do this?*

Strategy asks: *What are we trying to accomplish, and what choices give us the best shot?*

- **Planning** is about the steps you'll take.
- **Strategy** is about choosing which steps are worth taking, and why.

Let's say your school values reading engagement. You've noticed more students are choosing books over iPads. That's a promising sign. But strategy requires more than observing the shift; it asks you to test a theory:

> *If students are more engaged with reading, then we will see measurable growth in reading proficiency and their ability to read critically.*

If that's your theory, then the strategic work is to make it testable and actionable. For example:

- What evidence do we have that engagement is impacting the ability of our readers?
- How do we define and measure "reading proficiency" and "reading critically"?
- What initiatives are *intentionally* designed to increase reading engagement?
- Are these improvements happening because of something *we did*, or just by chance?

If engaged reading is a core value, then the strategic follow-up is: *What are we doing to activate that value in real, visible ways?*

Are we curating classroom libraries aligned with student interests?

Are we scheduling sustained silent reading and protecting that time?

Are we celebrating student reading lives publicly and regularly?

Are we tracking how often students choose to read, and what they choose to read?

This is the work of strategy. It turns values into evidence-informed choices. It moves us from good intentions to designed impact. It connects the dots between action and outcome. And most importantly, it holds us accountable, not just for what we *do*, but for what it *does* for students.

A One-Page Strategy Test

Try this: explain your school's strategy in one page, or better, in one conversation.

If you can't, you likely have a *wish list*, not a strategy.

A strong strategy is short, sharp, and specific. It's understandable by staff, explainable to parents, and visible in practice.

Ask yourself:

- Can your leadership team articulate the same strategy, without comparing notes?
- Do your resource allocations match your strategic priorities?
- Can you measure whether your strategy is working?

"You can't manage what you can't measure." - Peter Drucker.

It's not about being clever, it's about being clear.

Those who prioritize everything value nothing

Here's the paradox: strategy gives you freedom *because* it imposes limits.

When we chose to shift our softball defense, we also narrowed the range of defensive plays. That made it easier to train. It focused our players' awareness. It built confidence. Fewer variables meant clearer decisions.

Schools need the same discipline.

Strategy allows you to say:

- **Yes**, to initiatives that align with your theory of success.
- **No**, to distractions, even tempting ones.
- **Later**, to good ideas that don't fit *now*.

"Those who prioritize everything value nothing."

Strategic clarity reduces overload. It protects staff from initiative fatigue. It increases the chances that your efforts will stick. And it does something even more important: it allows us to stay focused on the future, not just the present.

I often ask educators to imagine the student who will graduate in 2036. That child is sitting in our classrooms today. The world they will enter is uncertain, but one thing is clear: they will need skills, mindsets, and resilience that go far beyond meeting today's standards. If we only react to the latest curricular requirement or assessment trend, we are already behind.

Schools should be places where visionaries plan for and shape the future we want, not just institutions that react to the demands of the moment. Strategy is what allows us to lift our eyes from the immediate to the long-term.

Carolyn, the student we are "building for the future," is not developed by chance. She is the product of intentional choices made by educators who aligned behind a clear strategy. That is the promise of strategic clarity: not just fewer initiatives, but better ones, the kind that give our students the future they deserve.

In Case You're Wondering, Yes, This Applies to Schools

Sometimes people push back and say, "But we're not a business." That's true. Schools operate in a very different context, centered on human development, not shareholder return. But that doesn't mean strategy doesn't apply. If anything, it makes the strategy more essential. Schools are stewards of learning, identity, and growth. They are accountable to a mission, to measurable outcomes, and most importantly, to the students and communities they serve.

In education, the stakes are too high to rely on guesswork or scattershot improvement efforts. A clearly defined strategy helps leaders focus on what will truly move the needle, guiding everything from instructional priorities to resource allocation. It ensures that professional learning, assessment design, and even community partnerships are pulling in the same direction.

Bernard Marr once said, "Doesn't matter how much data you have, it's whether you use it successfully that counts." The same is true for strategy. It's not about having 100 documents. It's about having one document that's actually used, one that aligns identity with action and connects intention to impact.

We aren't here to make profits. We're here to make a difference. Strategy is what helps ensure that difference is intentional, scalable, and sustained.

"A wealth of information creates a poverty of attention." - Herbert Simon

We don't need more ideas. We need *better choices*.

Vignettes from the Field: The Missed Moment of Book Week

Wendy, the school librarian, had poured her heart into Book Week. One of the key initiatives was a schoolwide challenge: students would log their reading minutes, classes would celebrate milestones, and the joy of reading would be visibly championed across the campus.

But the week didn't go as planned.

Teachers weren't tracking minutes. Some forgot entirely. Students weren't reminded to read or record. The initiative didn't land. Wendy felt let down, not by the kids, but by the energy that never materialized. "It felt like no one else was in it with me," she said.

In a conversation that followed, we unpacked what had happened. The problem wasn't the idea; Book Week is a great initiative. The problem was that it started with the *initiative*, not with the *strategy*.

What if we had begun differently?

- What if we had first defined the **WHO**, why does reading engagement matter to our school identity?
- What if we had clarified the **WHO**, what do we believe happens when kids are genuinely hooked on reading?
- What if we had gathered the team to articulate the impact *before* launching the activity?

A strategic approach might have shifted everything. By defining a theory of impact, *more reading engagement leads to greater growth in proficiency and critical literacy*, teachers may have seen themselves in the purpose, not just the task.

This is a reminder: Strategy doesn't start with activities. It starts with values, beliefs, and outcomes. When the WHO is clear, the WHAT has a better chance of sticking.

Strategy Is Also About the Future

If we zoom out, strategy isn't just about better decision-making today; it's about aligning with the world our students will face tomorrow.

We must ask hard questions:

- Is the current model of schooling truly preparing our students for the future they will inherit?
- Do our "strategic plans" reflect **future-back thinking**, starting with what's coming and working backward to today? Or are they just **present-to-**

future tweaks, attempts to patch an outdated system with a new language?

If we agree that our current education system, still deeply rooted in traditional structures, is not enough to meet future needs, then when do we *actually* change?

When do we stop adjusting around the edges and start building a new theory for how education works? One that is bold. Coherent. Aligned. Strategic.

That's the work ahead.

In the Next Chapter…

We'll walk through how to build your school's strategy using the **Bullseye Model**, a framework that helps you define your identity, map your current reality, and make deliberate choices about how to move forward.

Because strategy isn't about doing everything, it's about choosing the right things, for the right reasons, and doing them well.

We also need to think about the future and strategy. Do we agree that today's education, which is still quite traditional in nature, truly prepares our students for the future? Do our "strategic plans" reflect a future-back thinking or are they present to future thinking? If we agree that our current education system will not meet the future needs of students, when do we change, when do we become more theory-based in our approach instead of trying to tweak an already outdated system?

Chapter 3: From Drift to Direction

At the beginning of the school year, I was asked by senior leadership to contribute to a four-hour leadership retreat. "What's something meaningful you could bring to the table?" they asked. My answer? A strategic decision-making model to help bridge the gap between strategy and execution.

My line manager gave it the green light, and I got to work. I curated a set of key readings from Stacey Barr, especially her focus on measurable outcomes and the dangers of initiatives without evidence. "No change initiative is worth doing if we can have no evidence of whether it makes any kind of difference that matters," she writes. That idea became the foundation.

I built a simple, usable model around three pillars:

1. Desired Impact – What are we trying to achieve?

2. Measurement of Success – How will we know we're making progress?

3. Initiatives – What actions will get us there?

The session landed well. I walked the leadership team through it, connected it to our school's context, and challenged the "READY, FIRE, AIM" culture. When I finished, the room applauded. The feedback was positive. I was later invited to present the same model to the high school faculty, again, an ovation.

And then, nothing.

Despite early enthusiasm, the model never took root. I expected to walk into planning meetings and see it on the whiteboard, guiding our thinking. I thought it would become our common language. But after a few months, it faded. It appeared only when I presented it at external workshops or conferences, not in our own decision-making.

Teachers began asking, "What happened to that model?"

There was no clear answer.

And that's the real cost of not anchoring strategy in shared systems and structures.

The idea wasn't the problem.

The execution wasn't the problem.

The absence of organizational adoption, the lack of shared strategic clarity, was the problem.

Even great models drift when they aren't rooted in a system that supports them.

Organizational drift isn't inevitable, but it is predictable when strategy lives in slides instead of systems. To melt the iceberg, schools need to embed strategy into daily practice, not reserve it for retreats. That means revisiting core values regularly, evaluating progress of impacts on objectives, aligning resources with what matters most, and turning models into shared habits. It means asking tough questions before launching something new: Is what we are currently doing not working? Is this aligned with our desired impact? How will we measure if it works? Who owns the follow-through? Preventing drift requires more than good intentions; it demands discipline, alignment, and a commitment to learning forward, not just reacting backward.

The Courage to Choose

Strategy is not just about making better choices. It is about making the right choices, anchored in what we believe matters most for our students. It is not about doing more. It is about doing what matters, on purpose, with coherence.

When we fail to define our values and connect them to evidence and action, we drift. Even powerful ideas fade without structure. Even well-received models disappear without shared ownership. And even data becomes a distraction when it is not aligned to what we care about most.

But when we get the strategy right, when it is grounded in future-to-present thinking, rooted in a clear definition of success, and supported by the courage to say no to what does not fit, we create the conditions for meaningful impact.

We move from noise to signal.

From confusion to clarity.

From drift to direction.

The Strategic Anchor

The strategic anchor is what keeps us steady. It links our WHO (identity and values) with our WHERE (current context) and directs every WHY, HOW, and WHAT that follows. Without an anchor, schools are tossed from one initiative to the next, driven more by urgency or trends than by intention. With an anchor, schools filter choices through a shared lens: Does this align with who we are, where we are, and what we believe will matter most for our students in the future?

Just as Denmark anchored Klassens Tid in values of student empathy, agency, and belonging in 1993 and saw decades of payoff, every school must identify its own anchor. That anchor is the safeguard against drift. It is the point of clarity that transforms activity into strategy, and strategy into impact.

Anchoring the Future: Lessons from Klassens Tid

In 1993, Denmark made a bold strategic choice. Through the Folkeskole Act, they introduced Klassens Tid as a compulsory part of schooling. At first glance, it looked like simple scheduling: a weekly class meeting for teachers and students. But it was more than an activity. It was a deliberate, future-facing decision.

Denmark recognized that children entering school in 1993 would be middle-aged adults in 2025. They asked themselves: What kind of citizens will these six-year-olds need to be when they are forty?

Their answer was clear. Beyond literacy and numeracy, students would need empathy, agency, and belonging. They would need to practice dialogue, collaboration, and problem-solving. So Denmark built a structure where students could raise concerns, celebrate successes, and solve problems together. It was anchored in values (WHO), grounded in context (WHERE), designed with clear impact (WHY), structured for dialogue (HOW), and implemented as a weekly action (WHAT).

Thirty-two years later, we can see the results. Evaluations show that Klassens Tid has strengthened student well-being, improved teacher-student trust, reduced conflict, and increased participation in democratic life. Denmark's decision in 1993 was not just about meetings. It was about shaping the kind of adults their children would become.

Now we must ask: Are we making those same kinds of choices today?

What strategic bets are we willing to place for Carolyn, the student who will graduate in 2036?

- Will we anchor in values that go beyond test scores, such as agency, creativity, and resilience?
- Will we design structures that prepare her for adaptive readiness in a rapidly changing world?
- Will we measure what matters, not just what is easy to count?

Denmark's choice in 1993 reminds us that strategy is not about adding activities. It is about committing to a theory of success and embedding it deeply into practice. The question is whether we have the same courage today.

What Is Strategy, Really?

Let's be honest, schools confuse strategy with planning all the time.

We say we have a "strategic plan," but it's really a list of projects, initiatives, or aspirations. Not a theory. Not a choice. Not a commitment.

A working definition of strategy, drawn from Roger Martin, Michael Porter, and Rich Horwath, gives us a clearer formula:

Strategy is a set of choices that defines how you will be unique, how you will measure success, and what you will do to create that success.

It's not:

- A vision statement
- An aspiration to be "the best"
- A checklist of best practices
- A cautious attempt to please everyone

Instead, it is:

- Alignment across the organization
- Clear about what not to do
- Grounded in a shared language

- Designed to make hard choices about what matters most

In education, this means choosing what you value most, what you believe will have the greatest long-term impact on your students' ability to thrive in a future we cannot fully predict. Strategy is not just about choosing what to do; it's also about deciding what not to do. That's where clarity is born.

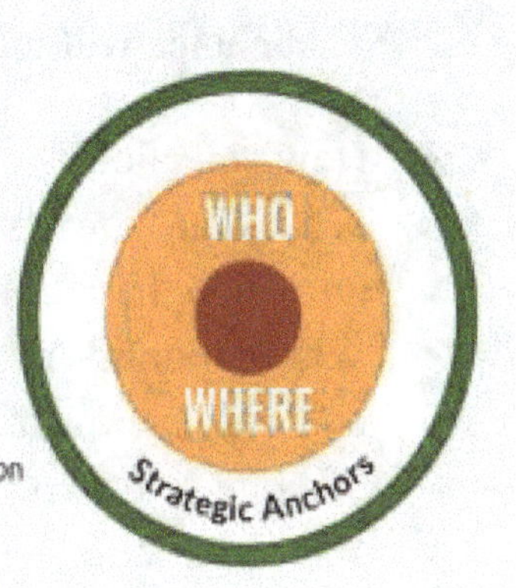

Future-to-Present Thinking: Anchoring to What Matters Most

Most schools operate with a present-to-future mindset: we look at what's currently happening, respond to data trends, and then set goals based on what's already in motion.

But strategy demands the reverse.

Future-to-present thinking is about deciding what kind of future you want to create, and then working backward to make decisions today that get you there. It's rooted in values and designed for impact.

Let's say your school believes that empathy, integrity, and resilience are the most critical character attributes your students need to thrive in a volatile, uncertain, complex, and ambiguous (VUCA) world. That belief isn't just a slogan; it becomes your strategic anchor.

That choice will influence:

- How you allocate resources, budget, time, training.
- What data you collect, are students demonstrating growth in these traits?
- What programs or pedagogies are prioritized? You don't just choose an SEL curriculum; you choose one that builds those values.
- Who you hire, teachers who embody and model those traits.
- Who you develop, teachers aligned with the mission, but needing support.
- Who you reward, those making the deepest impact on these outcomes.
- Who you release, those unwilling or unable to align with your chosen direction.

That's what strategy looks like:

Values → Choices → Focused Action → Measurable Impact.

Without this chain of logic, even well-intentioned decisions become misaligned, and organizational drift creeps in unnoticed.

Ready, Fire, Aim

The iceberg doesn't sink the ship because of what's visible above the surface; it's what's hidden below that causes the damage.

In schools, it's the same. You can be full of energy, launching initiatives, scheduling training, and investing in platforms. You look busy. But underneath? Disconnected effort. A false sense of progress. Scattered resources. A chronic lack of strategic clarity. That's when you hit the iceberg.

When planning leads without strategic direction, the organization stays busy but loses its way.

That's organizational drift, the inevitable outcome when we move without alignment, when we react to data rather than anchor ourselves to it, when we say "yes" without understanding our "why."

Why Drift Happens

If your process is:

- READY → FIRE → AIM, you're building drift into the DNA of your school.
- Waiting for trends in data before acting? You're already behind.

- Initiating programs before defining your anchor? You're layering confusion, not progress.

When schools operate like this, the symptoms show up quickly:

- Lack of Strategic Clarity: Nobody agrees on what success looks like.
- Scattered Resources: Budget, time, and energy get pulled in too many directions.
- False Sense of Progress: Busyness is mistaken for impact.
- Disconnected Effort: Teams work in silos, duplicating efforts or pursuing different goals.
- Organizational Drift: The school appears to move, but without purposeful direction.

The danger here isn't simply doing too much, it's doing too much without coherence. Initiatives become movement. Data becomes reactive. Talented people lose motivation when they no longer understand how their work connects to something meaningful.

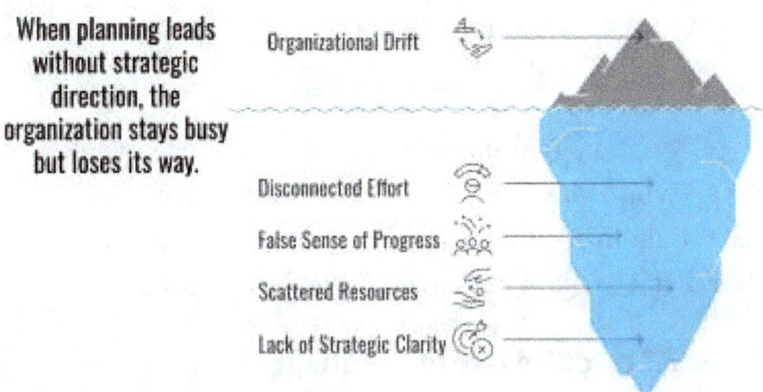

Figure 1b: Organizational drift is what happens when schools move with energy but without alignment. Like an iceberg, the danger lies beneath the surface. Disconnected effort, scattered resources, a false sense of progress, and a lack of strategic clarity. When the process is "Ready, Fire, Aim," busyness replaces impact, and schools lose their way.

The Bullseye Model: A Shared Anchor

To prevent drift, schools need a common language and structure. That's where the Bullseye Strategy Model comes in.

Start with the WHO: Who are we as a school? What do we stand for? What do we believe will be most impactful?

Then identify the WHERE: Where are the gaps in our practice? What needs attention?

Only then move to the WHY, HOW, and WHAT, your chosen objectives, approach, and initiatives.

When the WHO and WHERE are clear, everything else aligns.

When they're not, you're just firing in different directions and calling it momentum.

A strategy framework doesn't eliminate complexity; it gives you a way to manage it. It ensures that no matter how many initiatives, trainings, or projects are in motion, they're all moving in the same direction: toward impact.

But what if you're already drifting?

You'll notice it in the symptoms: repeated initiatives with no closure. Teams are working hard, but are unsure if they're working on the right things. Data was collected but rarely acted upon. Teachers are wondering what happened to last semester's "big focus." Drift sounds like, "We tried that already," or "I think someone's doing that, but I'm not sure who." It looks like a calendar full of meetings, but the staff is unsure of direction. When momentum replaces purpose, and when decisions are made from urgency rather than alignment, you're drifting. The good news? Once you name it, you can stop it.

Vignettes from the Field: Klassens Tid – Futures Job Report 2025

In 1993, Denmark made a bold move. Through the Folkeskole Act, they introduced Klassens Tid as a compulsory element of schooling. At first glance, it looked like simple scheduling: a weekly class meeting. But behind it was a strategic bet on the future.

Policymakers asked themselves a hard question: What kind of adults will today's six-year-olds need to be when they turn forty? Their answer was not limited to test results. It was about agency, dialogue, belonging, and collaboration. The human skills needed to thrive in a world that was rapidly changing.

Fast forward thirty-two years. The Future Jobs Report of 2025 confirms the wisdom of that choice. The most in-demand skills today are collaboration, problem-solving, adaptability, creativity, and emotional intelligence. These are exactly the traits Denmark deliberately embedded into its classrooms through weekly dialogues in Klassens Tid. What looked like a small scheduling decision in 1993 turned out to be a long-range strategy for shaping future-ready citizens.

Now, let's look ahead. Carolyn, the student who will graduate in 2036, is already in our classrooms. She will enter a world even more unpredictable than today's. One where artificial intelligence will be her co-pilot, climate and geopolitical instability will define her context, and entirely new industries will emerge.

The question for us is the same one Denmark asked in 1993: What kind of adult will Carolyn need to be when she turns forty?

If Denmark's bet paid off through agency, voice, and collaboration, what bets are we willing to place now?

- Will we anchor in values that go beyond compliance and test scores?
- Will we build structures that give Carolyn not just knowledge, but adaptability, resilience, and purpose?
- Will we design systems that measure what matters, not just what is easy to count?

Klassens Tid reminds us that strategy is not about activities. It is about committing to a coherent theory of success and embedding it deeply in practice. Denmark made those choices in 1993, and the Future Jobs Report of 2025 shows they were right. The challenge is whether we will do the same for Carolyn and her classmates, so that when they reach forty, they are not simply surviving in the world they inherit, but thriving in it.

Chapter Wrap-Up: From Drift to Direction

Schools do not fail because educators lack passion. They drift because passion without clarity scatters. A new initiative here, a training session there, another plan tucked into a binder, all good intentions, but without coherence. Drift feels busy. Drift looks active. Drift even earns applause at retreats. But drift does not last.

Strategy is the antidote. Not strategy as a slogan, or a checklist of projects, but strategy as a theory of success: anchored in identity and context, defined by what matters most, and disciplined enough to say no to what does not align. The strategic anchor keeps schools steady when trends pull hard and urgency tempts us off course.

Denmark understood this in 1993. Their choice to embed Klassens Tid was not about filling a timetable slot. It was a deliberate bet on the kind of citizens they wanted six-year-olds to become by the time they turned forty. Three decades later, the Future Jobs Report of 2025 validates that bet. The human skills most in demand are collaboration, adaptability, problem-solving, and emotional intelligence, and those were the very skills Denmark anchored into its classrooms.

That is the kind of strategic courage schools need today.

Carolyn will inherit a world more uncertain than ever. If we want her to thrive in it rather than simply survive, we must place our bets now. That means anchoring in values beyond compliance and scores. It means designing structures that nurture resilience and adaptability. It means measuring what matters, not just what is easy to count.

Drift will always be the default when strategy lives in slides instead of systems. Direction comes when strategy is lived out daily. In choices, in conversations, and in classrooms.

The challenge for us is simple: will we keep drifting, or will we anchor our schools to what matters most and move with purpose from drift to direction?

Coming Up: WHO and WHERE – Anchoring the Bullseye

In the next chapter, we dive into the Bullseye Strategy Model, a simple but powerful structure for building strategic clarity across your school. And it all starts with two deceptively simple questions:

- **WHO are we?**
- **WHERE are we now?**

Before you chase improvement, implement new tools, or roll out another initiative, you need to name your values and locate your starting point. Because if you don't know who you are or where you're standing, you'll never know if you're moving forward.

Reflection Prompt:

Think about your current school or team.

- Where do you see signs of organizational drift?
- Are your current initiatives clearly anchored to a shared strategy, or are they more like well-intentioned guesses?
- What is your school choosing not to do, and is that choice intentional?

Now take it further:

If you had to define your school's strategic anchor in one sentence, what would it be?

And if you can't… what needs to change?

Chapter 4: Anchoring Strategy – WHO and WHERE

A Half-Ironman, a Swim Crisis, and the Power of WHO + WHERE

A few years ago, my friend Andrew, Big Bear, challenged me to complete a 70.3 Half Ironman. Of course, I took up the challenge.

One small problem: I don't swim.

A bigger problem: not being able to swim in an Ironman doesn't just mean you might not finish; it means life might literally finish before the bike segment begins.

Now, I'm a strong cyclist and a decent runner. My instinct could've been to double down on those strengths and hope I just "got through" the water. But that's not a strategy. My Key Performance Indicator (KPI) was simple: finish the race, hopefully around 5.5 hours. But my foundational KPI was even more basic: don't drown.

So I built a strategy. I still trained for cycling and running, but the bulk of my time and resources went into swimming. Not improving it, learning it. I tracked my progress. The data showed I was becoming proficient enough. I could feel the difference. Confidence started to replace anxiety.

And then came race day.

What a terrible experience.

I got caught in the wave of faster athletes who started behind me. I was kicked, shoved underwater, and punched. I even got yelled at underwater, which I didn't realize was possible. Somehow, I came out of the water ten minutes faster than expected, which sounds great, except I was so disoriented that I completely fell apart in the transition zone. I fumbled around for twenty minutes before finally getting on my bike.

Never again.

But here's the point: I made it through. Not because I focused on what I was already good at, but because I anchored my plan in who I really was at the time (a non-swimmer) and where I was starting from (limited swim capability). I didn't ignore my other strengths; I just understood they wouldn't matter if I didn't first address what mattered most.

Schools often make the same mistake. They double down on strengths and gloss over gaps. That's not strategy. That's drift.

That's what strategy is: clear-eyed prioritization based on identity, context, and purpose.

Strategy Without Identity Is Directionless

You can't set a direction if you don't know two things: who you are and where you are.

That's why the first two steps of the Bullseye Strategy Model are the WHO and the WHERE. These aren't abstract ideas. They're your strategic anchor. They ground everything else, your goals, your initiatives, your metrics, and your actions.

Too often in schools, we leap straight into the WHAT, we launch programs, adopt platforms, and write action plans. But when those actions aren't rooted in a clear sense of identity or reality, we get movement without meaning.

> "Strategy is not planning. Strategy is about making choices, trade-offs; it's about deliberately choosing to be different." - Michael Porter

Trying to lead without knowing your WHO and WHERE is like climbing a ladder as fast as possible, only to realize it was leaning against the wrong wall.

Before we go further, let's clarify the difference.

- **WHO** is about identity: Who are we? What do we believe? What makes us unique? What kind of learners, and learning, do we stand for?
- **WHERE** is about reality: What's actually happening right now? What patterns are emerging? Where are we strong or stuck? How well are we doing?

Strategy needs both. WHO gives you direction. WHERE keeps you grounded. One without the other leads to either wishful thinking or reactive chaos.

The WHO – Defining Your School's Identity

WHO is the soul of your school. It's what you stand for. What makes you different. What you believe students need to thrive in a world that doesn't yet exist. "Who are we?"

When schools are clear on WHO they are, decisions feel focused. When they're not, every decision can lead you somewhere different.

Why WHO Matters

Your WHO gives meaning to your mission. It filters what you say yes to and what you politely decline. It connects every department, every level, and every initiative with a common thread. It aligns recruitment, culture, curriculum, assessment, and professional learning.

"A strategy must define what makes you unique. It must include what you are not going to do." - Rich Horwath, Strategic

"Without a clearly defined strategy, your organization is vulnerable to drift." - Roger Martin

WHO as Theory of Impact

Choosing your WHO is not about narrowing your focus at the expense of everything else. It's about identifying what you believe will generate the greatest positive ripple effect across your entire school.

It's the strategic bet you are willing to make.

In strategy terms, your WHO is a theory of impact. It's your if–then–because logic:

- **If** we focus on developing these specific values and capacities,
- **Then** we will see sustainable gains in learning, engagement, and student growth,
- **Because** these traits prepare students for a complex future and align with what our educators can consistently deliver when supported.

That bet should not be made in the comfort of where you are already strong. It should be made in the space where you most need to grow. The WHO is not a mirror of current strengths. It is a compass pointing toward your intended future.

What Are Strategic Anchors?
Anchors Define Who We Are and Where We Stand
Strategic Anchors are the core principles and focus areas that keep the school aligned and grounded in purpose.
In schools: WHO we are - our shared values. E.g., Empathy, Student Self-Direction, Well-being, and Literacy
They prevent organizational drift by aligning every initiative and decision to a shared purpose. They are the north stars that connect data, action and impact.
WHO
WHERE
ANCHORS
Anchors align belief with evidence — identity meets reality.

Future-to-Present Thinking

As Roger Martin reminds us: "Strategy requires thinking backward from a desired future state to the choices and capabilities needed now."

This is the essence of defining your WHO. Instead of designing your identity around today's habits or compliance demands, you ask: What kind of learners will thrive in the world ahead? What values, dispositions, and competencies will allow them to flourish?

Then you work backward, embedding those qualities into curriculum choices, staff hiring, data use, professional learning, and daily classroom practice. Your WHO becomes the lens that clarifies every decision.

The Lever Effect

Your WHO is not just an identity statement. It is your strategic lever, the point of force that amplifies impact across the system. Like Archimedes' principle, "Give me a place to stand and I will move the world." Your WHO gives you a place to stand, a focal point that turns small, aligned actions into significant, schoolwide change.

When your WHO is clear:

- **Resource Allocation**: Budgets, time, and energy flow to the priorities that amplify your chosen values, not to scattershot initiatives.

- **Professional Learning:** PD is not a menu of random opportunities but a cohesive investment in building the capacities teachers need to nurture your WHO.
- **Data Use:** Evidence is selected and tracked not because it is available, but because it directly tells the story of whether your WHO is becoming real.
- **Hiring and Development:** Staff are chosen, supported, and rewarded for their alignment with the identity you are intentionally cultivating.
- **Initiative Design:** New programs are not launched because they are fashionable, but because they directly move the needle on your WHO.

From Ideal to Performance Focus

The WHO is not an abstract ideal. It is a performance focus.

If you say empathy matters, then you measure it.

If you say resilience matters, then you track it.

If you say student agency matters, then your evidence must show it.

And because it is measured, it is managed. Initiatives stop being siloed projects and instead become levers designed to move the same needle. Over time, this coherence compounds. Teachers begin to see progress. Students begin to experience consistency. Families start to recognize the through-line of your identity.

The Anchor in Action

Denmark's decision in 1993 to anchor its schools in student agency and belonging through Klassens Tid was a WHO choice. They did not know exactly what the year 2025 would hold, but they bet that dialogue, voice, and collaboration would matter for their six-year-olds when they became forty. The Future Jobs Report of 2025 proved them right.

Your school faces the same challenge. Carolyn, graduating in 2036, will not thrive because we layered more activities onto her schooling. She will thrive because we dared to define a clear WHO, anchor to it, measure it, and align our actions around it.

Your WHO is not just your identity. It is your lever.

Your amplifier.

Your through-line.

Your safeguard against drift.

And your multiplier of impact.

If I Were Starting a School: My WHO Commitments

If I were starting a school from scratch, this is where I would place my strategic bet. These are the WHO statements, the values and capacities I believe, if done well, would create the most profound and lasting impact across all aspects of learning and development:

Strategic Focus Area	WHO Commitment	Measurables
Approaches to Learning (ATL)	We believe students who are strategic, reflective, and self-directed learners will be best equipped to adapt, problem-solve, and take ownership of their future.	% of students setting and reviewing personal learning goals • Frequency of student-led reflections in portfolios • Growth in student self-assessment accuracy vs. teacher assessment • Evidence of transfer of skills across subjects
Social-Emotional Learning (SEL)	We believe students who demonstrate empathy, resilience, and integrity build stronger communities, engage more meaningfully in learning, and thrive in the face of challenge.	•Student well-being survey scores (sense of belonging, resilience) • Number of peer-to-peer conflict resolutions without escalation • Participation rates in service or community projects • Teacher ratings of SEL growth on rubrics
Reading	We believe readers who are engaged, proficient, and	• % of students meeting or exceeding

	critical are empowered to make meaning of the world around them and to participate thoughtfully in complex discourse.	reading growth targets (MAP or other) • Time spent in voluntary/independent reading • Student engagement surveys on reading enjoyment • Assessments of critical reading (inference, bias detection, synthesis)
Mathematics	We believe students who are confident, fluent, and reasoned thinkers can apply mathematical understanding with flexibility, purpose, and clarity in real-life situations	• % of students meeting/exceeding math growth targets • Problem-solving tasks scored on reasoning rubrics • Student confidence ratings in math surveys • Evidence of application in real-world or cross-disciplinary projects
Wellness (Staff)	We believe staff wellness, including job satisfaction and a culture of belonging, is essential to sustainable	• Staff well-being survey results (workload, belonging, purpose) • Retention rates year-to-year • % participation in wellness initiatives

	performance and student success.	• Absenteeism and sick leave patterns
Professionalism	We believe professionalism means continual growth, deep accountability, and collaboration grounded in shared purpose.	• % of teachers engaged in professional learning communities (PLCs) • Evidence of peer observation and feedback cycles • Participation in external PD and certifications • Alignment of professional goals with schoolwide priorities

These aren't abstract mission statements; they're strategic, measurable commitments. Each one shapes what gets measured, what gets resourced, and what gets reviewed. They drive our initiatives, inform our assessments, and guide our professional learning. Our goal is to directly improve these capacities, track growth in each area, and ensure teachers are equipped and supported to cultivate these traits in every student.

Pitfalls When WHO Is Unclear

- Teams define success differently.
- Initiatives compete instead of connect.
- School values hang on walls, but not lived in classrooms.

- "Best practices" are adopted without asking, "Best for whom?"

When your WHO isn't shared and visible, people fill in the blanks with their own interpretations, and then wonder why alignment feels so elusive.

For Every Strategic Yes, There Needs to Be a Strategic No

Strategy is not only about what you will do. It is also about what you will refuse to do, even when those opportunities look attractive, popular, or easy. Every "yes" creates direction, but only when it is paired with the courage to say "no" to distractions, misalignments, and surface-level activity.

A strategic yes commits you to a value or capacity you believe will create a ripple effect across learning. For example:

- Yes to building student self-direction through Approaches to Learning.
- Yes to prioritizing empathy, resilience, and integrity through Social-Emotional Learning.
- Yes to cultivating joy and criticality in reading.
- Yes to building flexible reasoning in mathematics.
- Yes to protecting staff wellness as the foundation of student success.
- Yes to professionalism grounded in growth, accountability, and collaboration.

But every yes must be guarded by a matching strategic no:

- No to over-scaffolding that undermines independence.
- No to one-off SEL programs that live only in posters and assemblies.
- No to reducing reading to compliance tasks or test scores.
- No to drill-and-kill mathematics that values speed over reasoning.
- No to overwhelming staff with initiatives that scatter focus.
- No to professional learning that checks boxes instead of building capacity.

These "no's" are not acts of limitation. They are acts of protection. They shield your anchor from drift, ensuring your school does not dilute its energy across too many directions at once. They create the discipline to hold steady when the pressure to chase trends, please stakeholders, or add "just one more thing" is strong.

Saying yes sets the vision. Saying no creates the clarity to pursue it with coherence. Without the no, your yes is just another aspiration. With the no, your yes becomes strategy.

The Necessary Art of Strategic Abandonment

We have now defined our Bullseye. The core, unifying theory of our success. We know what matters most. The magnetic pull of this new clarity is powerful, but it is immediately met by an equally powerful force: the inertia of everything we are already doing. This is the moment where most strategies begin their slow death, not from a fatal flaw, but from a thousand competing commitments. The clutter of the past suffocates them.

This brings us to the most disciplined, and often the most difficult, act of strategic leadership: strategic abandonment. It is the conscious and deliberate decision to stop doing things that, while perhaps good and well-intentioned, are not central to our newly defined Bullseye. This isn't about quitting; it's about focus. It's about creating the time, energy, and resources necessary for our most important work to flourish. Every "yes" to the Bullseye must be funded by a "no" to something else.

Let's bring it back to Carolyn. We are designing a school to prepare her for a complex, unpredictable future. Every initiative, every program, every meeting, and every report we ask our teachers to complete is a demand on the finite resources that could be serving her. Now, we must hold each of these existing commitments up to the light of our new strategy and ask the hard, honest question: "Does this directly and powerfully contribute to the future we are building for Carolyn?"

If the answer is a clear, resounding "yes," it stays. If the answer is "maybe," "sort of," or "it used to," then we have a candidate for abandonment. Letting go of a beloved literacy program that is no longer aligned with our core strategy isn't a failure; it is a profound act of service to Carolyn. It's a declaration that we are more committed to her future than we are to our past. It's the difficult, grown-up conversation that turns a strategy on a page into a living, breathing reality for the students in our care. Without this discipline, we are just another school with a beautiful plan, drowned out by the noise of our own activity.

The WHERE – Knowing Your Starting Point

Once you've defined who you are, the next step is figuring out where you're starting from.

WHERE is not a judgment; it's a diagnosis. It's your current reality. Your system's health check.

"You can't manage what you can't measure." - Peter Drucker

Why WHERE Matters

You can't design a meaningful strategy if you don't understand the present. It's tempting to skip this part, especially when the pressure to act is high. But acting without context leads to wasted time, misaligned initiatives, and frustrated stakeholders.

Strategy isn't about moving fast; it's about moving in the right direction.

How to Define WHERE

Start by collecting honest, representative data. Use both:

- Quantitative (achievement, attendance, engagement, survey scores).
- Qualitative (teacher reflections, student voice, leadership insights).

Ask:

- What are we doing well?
- What's inconsistent or unclear?
- Where are the pain points?
- What patterns are emerging across divisions?

Importantly, involve people. This isn't just a spreadsheet exercise. Hold listening sessions. Review classroom artifacts. Map curriculum coverage. Conduct a policy review. Read the culture between the lines.

Culture as Context, Culture as Strategy

The real challenge in defining WHERE is not data collection. It is building the psychological safety that allows people to say what needs to be said. Teachers must feel free to surface inconsistencies, blind spots, and frustrations without fear of blame. Students must believe their voices matter and will not be ignored. Leaders must be willing to hear truths that make them uncomfortable.

This is where culture itself becomes strategy. A school that cultivates openness, trust, and shared responsibility will always have a more accurate picture of its reality. A school where staff feel silenced or defensive will always operate from distorted data.

Knowing WHERE you are requires courage. Not only to look at the numbers but to listen to the voices behind them. Because once you truly see your starting point, you can choose a path forward with clarity, coherence, and credibility.

WHO + WHERE = Your Strategic Launchpad

Once you've clarified WHO you are and WHERE you are, you've built the launchpad for everything that follows.

"Strategy is a coordinated and integrated set of choices that positions you to win." - Roger Martin

Think of it like GPS: your WHO is the destination, your WHERE is the blue dot. Without both, the best maps are useless.

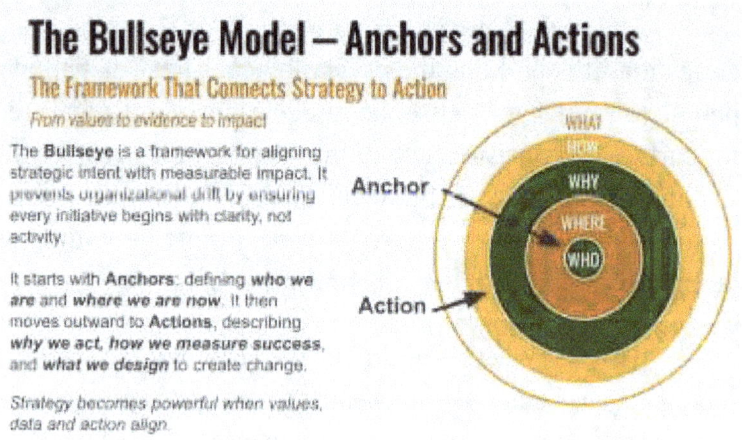

From Values to Evidence: Using WHO and WHERE to Guide the Data Strategy

Knowing your WHO and WHERE isn't just philosophical; it's the foundation for designing a strategic and data-informed system.

"If you can't measure an outcome, your initiatives won't impact that outcome." - Stacey Barr

Together, WHO and WHERE set the conditions for a structured, data-driven approach.

Structured Process for Establishing Data-Driven Instruction (Preview)

As the strategy unfolds in the next chapters, we'll explore how schools can systematically design and implement data-driven instruction. Here's a preview of that process:

1. Define Strategic Goals & Objectives
   o What do we value in this area of learning?
   o What are our objectives for student growth next year?
2. Establish Data Objectives
   o What needs to be tracked?
   o What data shows us where we are, and what we value?
   o What are our KPIs?

3. Identify the Right Data Tools
   o Match tools to data objectives (e.g., MAP Growth, classroom rubrics, SEL inventories).
4. Build Data Literacy
   o Train teachers to interpret data and act on it meaningfully.
   o Create PLCs focused on evidence-driven improvement.
   o Establish data cycles and feedback loops.

Your values define your measures.

Your current reality defines your focus.

Your strategy defines what happens next.

Chapter Wrap-Up: From Identity to Evidence

The Half-Ironman reminded me of a simple truth: strategy is not about doubling down on strengths; it is about identifying what really matters most in order to move forward. I did not need to be a faster runner; I needed to become a competent swimmer. The same principle applies to schools. We cannot leap into initiatives or programs until we know who we are and where we are.

WHO is the identity anchor. It defines the values and capacities we believe will have the deepest ripple effect on student learning and long-term growth. It is the strategic bet we make on the kind of people we want our graduates to become.

WHERE is the reality check. It grounds us in evidence, voices, and patterns so we do not build strategy on wishful thinking. It demands honesty, courage, and the psychological safety to name both strengths and gaps.

Together, WHO and WHERE form the launchpad for everything that follows. They give schools the clarity to filter opportunities, the discipline to say no to distractions, and the confidence to measure what truly matters. Without them, schools confuse movement for progress. With them, schools build coherence, alignment, and direction.

But here is the danger: if we stop at WHO and WHERE, if we define our identity and diagnose our context but fail to act with evidence, we risk slipping into the same trap schools have fallen into for decades: reacting instead of leading. And just as dangerous is jumping too quickly into the WHAT. Without grounding in WHO and WHERE, even well-intentioned actions become part of the drift. Activity without strategy, movement without meaning.

The next layer of strategy is about movement. Not just any movement, but intentional, disciplined, evidence-informed movement. In schools, that means using data not as a mirror to the past but as a tool to shape the future.

That is where we turn next. Chapter 5 will look at why so many schools remain stuck in descriptive analytics, why data literacy is often overestimated, and how this contributes to organizational drift. We will confront the limits of surface-level data use and offer a path toward deeper, more strategic analytics.

The guiding question will be simple, but powerful: What data are we collecting, and is it truly moving us toward what we say we value?

Only when we can answer that with clarity will we build strategies that not only look bold on paper, but also stick in practice.

Next: Chapter 5 – Data, Drift, and the Dunning-Kruger Dilemma

Chapter 5: Rearview Metrics, Curvy Roads

"Hi, Toilet!", A Data Lesson from Beijing

When I first moved to Beijing, I was eager to immerse myself in the culture, and that included learning the language. Like many newcomers, I started picking up phrases from friends. No formal lessons, just bits of conversational Chinese I could throw into daily life. It felt efficient. I wasn't aiming for fluency, just usefulness.

One of my closest friends in China, Troy, nicknamed "3-minute Wonder", spoke excellent Mandarin. He gave me two essential phrases to get started:

- **"Zǎo shàng hǎo" (Good morning)**
- **"Xǐ shǒu jiān zài nǎ?" (Where is the bathroom?)**

Armed with these, I began practicing every day. Each morning, I'd pass the security guard at my apartment and beam, "Nǐ hǎo, xǐ shǒu jiān!" (Hello, toilet!)

He always looked at me strangely but gave a polite nod. I assumed it was my poor pronunciation or wrong tone. Mandarin is a tonal language; say the same syllables with a different tone and you've said something completely different. I knew this in theory, but I didn't really know it.

A few days later, I was at a restaurant with Troy. He went to order food, and I needed to use the bathroom. So I turned to the waitress and asked, with full confidence:

"Zǎo shàng hǎo zài nǎ?" (Good morning is where?)

She looked at me, confused.

"Bù kě yǐ," she said. "You can't,"

I asked again. She smiled and replied, "Míng tiān kě yǐ." "Tomorrow, you can."

Now I was confused. Why would the bathroom be closed until tomorrow?

When Troy returned, I told him the bad news: "I think the bathroom's shut until tomorrow." He raised an eyebrow, asked the waitress a quick question, and then burst out laughing.

Turns out, I had completely reversed the two phrases.

I'd been cheerfully greeting the guard every morning by saying:

"Hello, toilet!"

And at the restaurant, I asked the waitress:

"Good morning is where?"

The lesson?

Just because I had memorized the phrases didn't mean I knew how or when to use them. I didn't understand the structure, the context, or the intent behind the language.

Without those, my well-intentioned attempts weren't just ineffective, they were confusing or even counterproductive.

It's exactly the same with data.

The Connection to Data

Educators often collect data like I collected phrases: scattered, disconnected, and without clear context. They might know the terms, MAP RIT scores, growth trends, and standard deviations, but without understanding what the data means, how to use it, or why it matters, the result is confusion at best and misinterpretation at worst.

It's not enough to have the data. You need to know:

- **Why** you're collecting it.
- **What decisions** it's supposed to inform.
- **How** to interpret it within the context of your school, your students, and your "WHO".

Without that, we risk walking around enthusiastically shouting "Hello, toilet!" thinking we're being strategic when we're actually just creating noise.

As Mark Twain said:

"Data is like garbage. You'd better know what you are going to do with it before you collect it."

Otherwise, we're just piling up phrases or spreadsheets, without a strategy.

Before we move into the strategic engine of WHY, HOW, and WHAT in the next chapter, it's important to pause. We've established WHO we are and WHERE we currently stand. But before charting our course forward, we need to talk about one of the most misunderstood foundations of strategic leadership: data. Understanding data, not just reading it, but using it with purpose, is one of the most crucial skills for any school leader. Yet, many schools struggle with this. This chapter explores why.

I've sat in leadership meetings where someone gestures to a graph and declares, "There's a trend here." Suddenly, that trend becomes a new initiative. A new focus. A new urgency. But no one stops to ask: What value are we trying to move toward? What does this trend mean in the context of our identity, our purpose, or our long-term goals? It's like noticing the wind has shifted direction and immediately changing course without asking where we're going in the first place.

This chapter is about that mistake.

The Mirage of Trends

School leaders are hungry for answers, and data seems to offer them. But too often, the way we use data is like chasing mirages. We see a pattern in a dashboard and leap into action. But action without direction isn't strategy, it's drift.

When we rely on surface-level patterns without anchoring them to our school's strategic identity, we lose focus. Every new "trend" becomes a reason to pivot, and before long, we're spinning in place. We may be busy, but we're not making progress.

As Herbert Simon warned:

"A wealth of information creates a poverty of attention."

The more data we have, the more tempted we are to respond to everything. But strategy requires focus. And focus means ignoring some things so you can double down on what matters most.

That's what this chapter is about.

Let's talk about how schools drift, and how data, used intentionally, can anchor us instead.

The Dunning-Kruger Dilemma

In my role, I've had the opportunity to engage deeply with the intersection of educational leadership, organizational behavior, and data analytics. With an MBA focused on strategic management and a professional certification in data analysis, I've spent years working to bridge the gap between vision and evidence. I've sat in countless meetings with school leaders, thoughtful, experienced professionals, eager to use data to make better decisions. And yet, more often than not, I hit a wall.

They tell me, "I love data."

They tell me, "I know data."

They tell me, "I've read Street Data."

And I believe them, genuinely. It's heartening that data is now part of the professional vocabulary in education. That's a significant shift from even a decade ago. But there's also a growing challenge: when familiarity is mistaken for fluency. Exposure to data is not the same as the ability to use it strategically. And this is not a criticism, it's a cognitive trap we're all susceptible to.

The Dunning-Kruger effect reminds us that people with limited knowledge in a domain often overestimate their expertise. In education, where data is increasingly visible, dashboards, survey results, test scores, and confidence can outpace competence. Leaders speak the language of data, but when it comes to aligning that data with strategy, designing interventions, or tracking impact, the gaps become visible.

Let's be clear: Street Data is a powerful and necessary contribution to our understanding of the learner experience. It centers voice, identity, and context. It challenges us to slow down and listen. But quoting Street Data, referencing anecdotal insights, or pointing to a few student comments is not the same as building a data strategy. It's not the same as knowing how to validate patterns across multiple data sets or make high-leverage decisions in real time.

Street Data lives closer to the qualitative, empathetic layer of the data landscape. It is essential. But strategy demands integration. It asks that we bring those insights into a structured decision-making model, one that honors voice while still pursuing outcomes.

Jordan Morrow defines data literacy as "having comfort and confidence to utilize data to help you make smarter, more intelligent decisions." He expands on this by naming the real skill: the ability to read, work with, analyze, and communicate with data. That's the level we must aspire to. Not just discussing what the data says, but understanding what it means, why it matters, and how to act on it.

Everyone starts somewhere. And loving data is a great place to begin. But strategic leadership calls for something more. It calls for clarity, discipline, and the humility to keep learning. Because ultimately, it's not about whether we value data, it's about whether we know how to lead with it.

Stuck in Descriptive

Most schools never move beyond the first, and most basic, level of data use: descriptive analytics. They can tell you what happened. How many students failed. What percentage of teachers reported low engagement. What was the average MAP score in the spring. This kind of data is helpful; it's necessary. But it's also limited.

To truly lead with data, schools need to understand the four levels of analytics. Each level serves a distinct purpose and requires a progressively deeper capacity for interpretation and action.

Level	Action Verb	Key Question	What It Does	Typical Use in Schools
Descriptive	*Observe*	What happened?	Summarizes and reports past data	Common and overused
Diagnostic	*Understand*	Why did it happen?	Explores causes and contributing factors	Rarely used systematically
Predictive	*Anticipate*	What might happen next?	Projects future outcomes	Almost never explored
Prescriptive	*Act*	What should we do about it?	Recommends targeted actions	Largely unknown or inaccessible

Descriptive data is comfortable. It's low risk and easy to access. But staying there makes us reactive. We're always a step behind, responding to symptoms instead of addressing causes. Schools that rely only on descriptive data find themselves in a constant state of adjustment, shifting gears based on what just happened rather than where they're trying to go.

This is why future-back thinking is so difficult. When strategy starts with "What did the data say last quarter?" instead of "What do we want to be true in 10 years?" we trap ourselves in a loop of present-to-future planning. The problem is that the future moves faster than we do.

And yes, this habit often leads schools to abandon initiatives too early. When progress does not show up in the first round of descriptive numbers, leaders pivot to the next big idea. Programs are dropped before enough time has passed to truly measure whether they are working. Staff become conditioned to wait out the latest initiative, assuming it will fade before results are visible.

Now imagine if Denmark had done that in 1993. Suppose the first surveys on Klassens Tid had shown uneven results, or teachers complained that students were slow to engage in structured dialogue. Without clear metrics for what mattered: student agency, belonging, conflict resolution, and trust. Would they have abandoned it at the first sign of adversity? If they had, the decades of impact we see today would never have materialized.

That is exactly the challenge for Carolyn of 2036. If we only judge initiatives on quick, descriptive wins, we risk pulling the plug before long-term benefits can emerge. Carolyn needs us to play the long game. She needs us to define, measure, and hold steady to the deeper outcomes that will prepare her for a world of AI co-pilots, climate instability, and industries not yet imagined.

Denmark bet on values that would outlast trends. The question is whether we will do the same for Carolyn. Or whether we will keep reacting to short-term data, changing direction before we ever give strategy a chance to work.

Case Study: When Innovation Outran Strategy

"Build the plane while flying it."

At a well-established international school, I was part of the design team for FLOW21, the Future of Learning initiative. On paper, it was ambitious. Students would design their own school days, booking themselves into sessions across math, science, and other subjects. We built a digital booking platform, created video tutorials for every math lesson, wrote online formative checkpoints, and offered open sessions for help. In science, students designed their own experiments, scheduled lab time, and completed MYP assessments as they went.

The energy was high, the innovation impressive, and many students loved the flexibility. Parents praised the independence their children were developing. One even remarked, "I cannot think of anything more powerful than introducing our kids to the idea that they have control of their own futures."

Looking back, it seemed clear that independence and self-direction were the intended outcomes of FLOW21. But without defining what "independence" meant or how we would measure it, the goal remained a loose aspiration. For example, we could have tracked whether students successfully followed their own schedules, met checkpoints on time, or demonstrated improved time-management skills compared to a baseline. Instead, independence was celebrated in anecdotes, not evidenced in data.

This stood in stark contrast to the previous three years, when our math and science teams had carefully rebuilt the middle school curriculum. By the end of that work, over 95% of our recommendations for extended math placement matched actual student success, and high school teachers consistently praised the improved preparation of their incoming students. Those were measurable gains.

With FLOW21, we were told to "build the plane while flying it." The initiative became a powerful lesson in how even exciting, well-resourced projects can drift without clarity. Students may have enjoyed the experience, but as a school, we could not answer the questions parents, teachers, or even students themselves asked about its real impact. For me, this was the first time I saw the difference between an initiative and a strategy.

"I don't know what it is…But I know that wasn't it."

The same pattern played out again when we were asked to design something like Genius Hour. Ray, our Design teacher, led the charge. He was passionate, and a team of six of us worked with him. We spent weeks researching, planning, and gathering data to show how it could deepen student engagement and creativity. The presentation Ray gave to the FLOW21 Director was outstanding. Thoughtful, inspiring, and evidence-based.

The response left us stunned: *"That was a wonderful presentation. It was thoughtful, inspiring, and well put together. However, it's not what I had in mind. I don't know what it is…But I know that wasn't it."*

The air went out of the room. Ray was devastated. The rest of us were deflated. Weeks of careful work, grounded in evidence, were dismissed not on their merits but on the Director's undefined vision. The problem wasn't the quality of the idea. It was the absence of anchoring objectives or criteria for success. Without those, even strong proposals could be rejected on a whim.

Had FLOW21 been framed through a strategic lens, the intended outcome of independence could have been anchored like this:

- Desired Impact: Students develop greater independence and self-direction in managing their learning.
- Measurement of Success: % of students meeting checkpoints without teacher reminders; average improvement in self-assessed time-management skills; teacher logs showing fewer missed sessions.
- Initiatives: Digital booking system with auto-tracking; weekly reflection surveys on independence; mentor check-ins coded for proactive vs. reactive support.

Anchored this way, FLOW21 would have moved from an inspiring idea to a measurable strategy. Independence wouldn't just be praised in anecdotes; it would be evidenced in data, guiding refinement and proving whether the model worked.

FLOW21 *was my first clear lesson in what happens when bold ideas run ahead of evidence. Innovation without anchoring objectives or measures becomes drift. It is a perfect example of how schools, caught in the comfort of descriptive stories rather than strategic evidence, mistake activity for progress. The cost of low analytics maturity is exactly this: time, talent, and energy poured into initiatives that generate stories but not evidence. Without clear measures, schools can't know whether they are advancing or simply circling the runway.*

The Cost of Low Analytics Maturity

In many schools, data use feels like progress, but without data literacy, it is just motion. Dashboards are created, tools are purchased, and reports are generated. But when you look closer, the real gap is not access to data; it is the ability to understand and use it with purpose. Too often, leaders and teachers lack the training to move beyond surface-level description. Without a shared framework for interpretation, the same set of numbers can tell a dozen different stories, allowing people to cherry-pick whichever one fits their narrative. Data without literacy does not create strategy, it makes noise. Strategic data use requires confidence, skill, and a disciplined process that turns evidence into alignment, not ambiguity.

This disjointed approach happens for a few reasons. Most leaders have not been trained in deep data literacy. They are comfortable reading reports, but not always equipped to analyze the patterns behind them or ask whether the data is measuring what truly matters. There is limited understanding of more advanced analytics: diagnostic, predictive, and prescriptive, and how these levels can shift a school from reactive to strategic. Even when data cycles exist, they are often rolled out without clearly defined objectives, leading to fragmented interpretations. The result is a system that unintentionally reinforces organizational drift instead of strategic alignment.

I experienced this tension firsthand. I was asked to map out the data literacy sessions I would hold for teachers this school year. On the surface, it seemed like a simple request. But when I began planning, it exposed a much deeper problem. How could I design meaningful sessions when our strategic anchors had not been established? We had plenty of data, but no clarity on which data mattered most or why. Without defined objectives, I would only be training teachers to interpret numbers in the dark.

In a conversation with the senior leadership team, I asked a simple but telling question: If we agree that meeting predicted growth in MAP Growth is one of our primary measures of success, then how do we want to use the data? From that single anchor, the path forward became clear:

- **School Level:** Identify overall strengths and weaknesses in instructional areas.
- **Division Level:** Target grade-level trends by domain, not just overall scores.
- **Teacher Level:** Adjust classroom instruction to explicitly address MAP domains.
- **Intervention Level:** Form small groups by instructional area need (e.g., vocabulary support, informational text comprehension).

If that decision had been made, I could have designed targeted data literacy sessions aligned to our strategy. But no decision was made. The anchors were missing. And without anchors, professional learning on data becomes another compliance exercise rather than a lever for impact.

This is the paradox many schools face: they want teachers to be "data literate," but they fail to define the purpose, outcomes, or objectives of the data itself. Without that clarity, data literacy cannot be taught, and strategy cannot take root.

Beyond Comfort: True Data Leadership

It's time for a mindset shift. Instead of proudly declaring, "We use data," the real question should be, "How are we using data to move toward our values?"

True data leadership begins with curiosity. It starts by asking sharper questions and challenging the assumptions behind the numbers. It requires us to develop our capacity to engage with all levels of analytics, not just describe what happened, but also investigate why it happened, anticipate what might come next, and determine what should be done.

And it calls for humility. Sometimes we simply don't know what the data is telling us, and that's okay. What matters is the willingness to learn, to seek clarity, and to align our interpretation of the data with the outcomes we care most about. Data leadership isn't about having all the answers; it's about creating the conditions to find them.

It also means acknowledging that comfort with data doesn't always equal fluency. There's no shame in that, only opportunity. When we recognize the limits of what we know, we open the door to meaningful growth.

As W. Edwards Deming said, "Without data, you're just another person with an opinion." But with the wrong use of data, you may be just another person drifting in the flow of trends.

Steadying the Compass: Using Data to Navigate Beyond the Cycle

The next time someone points to a data trend in a meeting, it's worth pausing before jumping into action. It's tempting to respond quickly, especially when the numbers seem to indicate urgency. A drop in engagement scores, a dip in achievement levels, or a spike in absenteeism can feel like flashing warning lights demanding immediate intervention. But not every signal is a siren. And when we move from one trend to the next without a guiding strategy, we risk becoming reactive leaders, rather than intentional ones.

Instead of treating every uptick or downturn as a call to arms, we must learn to interrogate the data before acting. We need to ask: What does this trend really mean? Is it connected to our broader vision? Is it something we expected, or something that challenges our current theory of change? Does it confirm our assumptions, or does it require us to revisit them?

The strategic leader resists the urge to respond impulsively. Instead, they look for alignment. Is this trend consistent with our values and our intended outcomes? Will responding to it help us move closer to the kind of school we want to be, or will it pull us off course? These aren't easy questions, but they're essential. Because without this level of discipline, we risk confusing motion with progress.

There's another risk, too: when leaders repeatedly pivot based on short-term data, they unintentionally train staff to wait out every initiative. Educators become accustomed to seeing new programs launched in response to last month's numbers, only to be replaced by next month's focus. Over time, this erodes trust. It reinforces a belief that change is temporary and driven by reaction, not by purpose.

To avoid this cycle, we need to use data not as a compass that spins with every gust of wind, but as a tool that helps us stay the course. Descriptive analytics can tell us what happened, but that's just the first level. We need to go deeper. Diagnostic analytics allow us to understand why something happened, uncovering root causes and systemic patterns. Predictive analytics help us anticipate future outcomes based on current trends. Prescriptive analytics guide us toward the best course of action, using evidence and modeling to inform decisions.

Using all four levels of analytics is not just a technical skill; it's a leadership mindset. It requires slowing down before speeding up. It asks us to be curious before being certain. And it reminds us that the goal is not to chase every data point but to pursue a defined impact with discipline and intentionality.

So the next time someone says, "There's a trend," ask:

- Does this align with our strategic priorities?
- What is the deeper story behind the data?
- Are we using the right level of analysis to understand and respond?
- Will acting on this help us move from where we are to where we want to be?

This shift, from reacting to projecting, from chasing trends to choosing purpose, is what separates tactical management from strategic leadership. It's how we begin to lead schools with coherence, clarity, and confidence. Ask:

- Is this trend aligned with our strategic intent?
- What is the outcome we are trying to achieve?
- What level of analytics have we engaged in?
- Are we reacting to what is, or moving toward what could be?

Descriptive analytics will always be a part of our work. But it cannot be the whole.

If we want to lead schools toward a more intentional, future-focused practice, we must step into diagnostic, predictive, and prescriptive territory. That's how we move from drift to discipline.

Data Audits: From Collection to Purpose

All of this brings us to a critical but often overlooked exercise: the data audit.

Schools collect enormous amounts of data, such as attendance records, assessment scores, reading levels, student feedback, and benchmark reports. But how much of it is actually being used to drive decisions that are clearly linked to a stated value or strategic objective? How much of it is guiding the school's direction rather than simply being reported?

A data audit is not just a technical inventory. It is a strategic reflection. It asks three essential questions:

1. What data are we collecting?
2. Who is using it, and for what purpose?
3. Is this data connected to a clearly defined value or outcome?

Consider reading as an example. Suppose one of our stated values is building critical literacy skills, and our desired impact is that students become proficient in reading for inference. In that case, we must ask: Do we have data that measures inference? Are we interpreting that data correctly? Are we spending time collecting other reading data that does not actually help us answer that question? If so, why are we collecting it at all?

This is how we begin to define our WHY. Not in general terms, but specifically. This data is linked to this data objective, which is aligned with this strategic value.

This connects directly to the Book Week example. That initiative fizzled not because it was poorly designed, but because its purpose and measures were never clearly established. Reading minutes were tracked, but they were not linked to larger outcomes such as engagement, comprehension, or growth in critical literacy. Without a clear data objective, Book Week became symbolic rather than strategic.

A data audit helps us avoid that mistake. It ensures that initiatives like Book Week do not just create activity, but actually connect to evidence, purpose, and impact.

And this matters because of students like Carolyn. When she looks back on her schooling, she will not remember how many pages she read in one themed week. What will shape her future is whether initiatives were designed and measured in a way that built her capacity to be a critical, engaged, and resilient learner. If Denmark had not tied Klassens Tid to clear values and evidence, it might have been abandoned at the first sign of difficulty. Instead, its persistence has shaped generations of students.

A data audit is how we safeguard Carolyn's future. It ensures that every program, every initiative, and every cycle of assessment is not just activity for its own sake but part of a coherent design to develop the dispositions she will need to thrive in 2036 and beyond.

When our data strategy begins with values, rather than availability, we can finally break the cycle of trend-chasing. We stop drifting and we start designing.

Chapter Wrap-Up: Conducting a Strategic Data Audit

Schools often collect vast amounts of data: student assessments, well-being surveys, behavior incidents, teacher reflections, MAP scores, internal benchmarks, rubrics, and observations. But the real question is not how much we collect. It is whether the data is being used to drive decisions that are truly aligned with our values and goals.

A strategic data audit helps answer that question. It is not just an inventory of information but a reflection on purpose and alignment. A simple SWOT-style approach can guide the process:

Area	Guiding Questions
Strengths	What data are we collecting that clearly supports our school values and drives informed decisions?
Weaknesses	What data are we collecting that rarely informs decisions? Are we duplicating efforts or collecting out of habit?
Opportunities	What values or objectives (e.g., reading for inference) lack strong supporting data? What could be developed or refined?

Threats	Are current data practices causing drift? Are we reacting to trends without a clear purpose?

Take reading as an example. If one of your values is developing critical literacy and your objective is to improve analytical reading skills, the audit asks: Do we have data that measures this? Are we interpreting it correctly? Are we spending time on other reading data that does not advance this goal? If so, why?

This is not a minor exercise. It is how we prevent initiatives from fizzling into one-off events. Think back to Book Week. Without clear metrics or a link to long-term literacy goals, it became symbolic rather than strategic. A data audit would have ensured it was measured against outcomes that mattered, such as engagement in critical reading, so that it contributed to lasting growth instead of a temporary burst of activity.

And this matters most for students like Carolyn. She will not be defined by how many books she read in a themed week, but by whether her school used evidence to design experiences that built her into a critical, engaged, and resilient learner. A strategic data audit ensures that every initiative she encounters is connected to the values and capacities her future will demand.

When schools commit to data audits, they create coherence. They move from collecting information for its own sake to building a disciplined strategy that links evidence with identity and purpose. That is the difference between drifting with trends and designing for impact.

In the next chapter, we will turn to the engine that powers this alignment: defining the WHY, crafting the HOW, and selecting the right WHAT.

Chapter 6: The Action in Strategy

Why the Bullseye Doesn't Begin with What

At some point, someone in the meeting will pull out a marker, draw three circles, and say, "Let's start with the WHY."

They're quoting Simon Sinek's Golden Circle, a popular model that flips traditional thinking on its head: don't start with what you do. Start with why you do it. What's your purpose? What's your belief?

It sounds right. It looks strategic. But here's the thing most schools miss:

If you haven't defined your WHO or understood your WHERE, then your WHY has no foundation.

That's like planning a mission to Mars without knowing where your rocket is launching from. It's vision without orientation. Intent without identity.

And without those anchors, most schools end up skipping right to the WHAT, because it's comfortable. It's visible. It's fast. But it's not strategy. It's reaction.

Why Strategy So Often Starts in the Wrong Place

A leadership team brought in a consulting group.

There wasn't a clear plan for them, no strategic brief, no defined outcomes. But the contract had already been signed, and the budget was committed, so they moved forward. The consultants did what consultants do: they ran focus groups, distributed surveys, and compiled findings on the school's organizational culture.

What they uncovered was deeply concerning.

The data painted a picture of a culture under strain. Teachers reported feeling uncomfortable speaking up in meetings, not out of apathy, but fear. Fear of being labeled difficult. Fear of being reprimanded. Fear of being excluded from decisions or future opportunities. The word "intimidated" came up more than once. So did "unsafe." And "silenced."

These weren't outliers. They were patterns.

Morale was low. Trust was fractured. Professional vulnerability, the kind that enables growth and honest collaboration, had been replaced by self-protection. People were nodding in meetings and venting in hallways. They were playing it safe, not because they didn't care, but because they didn't feel secure enough to care out loud.

So what did leadership do?

They launched Community Conversation Circles (CCCs).

Sixteen of them.

In theory, the idea sounded responsive. Leaders would make themselves available to hear staff feedback in a more casual setting, an open-door opportunity for dialogue.

But in practice, the execution missed the mark entirely.

Staff were told which topics could be discussed: "budgeting," "facilities," and "specific divisional initiatives." Conversations about culture, leadership behaviors, communication breakdowns, or psychological safety were not on the menu.

These weren't listening sessions. They were managed conversations, and everyone knew it.

Of the sixteen sessions, two had zero attendees. Ten had fewer than two people show up. In a school with over 200 faculty members, that's not just low engagement, it's an act of quiet resistance.

Staff weren't too busy. They weren't uninterested. They were making a statement:

"You're not really listening. You're controlling the narrative."

It wasn't silence.

It was disengagement.

It was refusal.

Because the real issue wasn't a lack of opportunity to speak.

It was a lack of safety to be heard.

The missteps were clear:

- Leaders never asked staff what they needed. There was no co-construction, no shared ownership. A solution was designed without the people who lived the problem.

- Leaders never assessed whether the initiative worked. No baseline, no follow-up, no reflection. The initiative wasn't strategic. It was just… done.

And here's the critical miss:

If the WHO had been defined upfront, something like:

"We believe staff wellness, job satisfaction, and a culture of belonging are essential to sustainable performance and student success," then everything would have looked different.

That anchor would have framed a theory of change:

If we invest in psychological safety, inclusion, and authentic voice.

Then we will see stronger collaboration, improved morale, and better student outcomes.

With that clarity, the leadership team might have asked different questions:

- How safe do staff currently feel to share concerns?

- What barriers prevent authentic dialogue?

- What behaviors or systems are unintentionally silencing staff?

They might have designed a different **WHAT:**

- Small-group culture conversations co-led by neutral staff.

- Anonymous input channels with transparent follow-up cycles.

- Empathy interviews with disengaged staff.

- Clear protection against retaliation for speaking up.

And they would have defined a meaningful **HOW:**

- Percentage of staff reporting psychological safety in surveys.

- Changes in voluntary participation over time.

- Qualitative shifts in feedback themes.

- Observable changes in leadership communication.

When the WHO is clear, the WHY becomes shared, the HOW becomes visible, and the WHAT becomes powerful. Without it, good intentions collapse into failed tactics.

A broken culture was met with a managed conversation.

An opportunity for healing turned into a case study in disconnection.

The real miss was not the CCCs. It was that the school had not anchored itself in WHO. One belief, defined at the start. Staff wellness, job satisfaction, and belonging are non-negotiables for student success, and that shift could have changed everything.

From Listening Once to Listening That Lasts

This wasn't just about failed conversations; it was about the absence of a strategy. Without structures and measures, even promising initiatives disappear.

When the school first introduced the circles, the idea carried promise. Teachers hoped it would signal a new culture of openness and belonging. But eight months later, nothing more was said. At the following year's professional development days, leaders presented on "belonging uncertainty." Was this linked to the concerns raised in those circles? We never knew. Two months into the year, both the circles and the belonging theme had quietly disappeared.

Belonging Uncertainty Explained

Belonging uncertainty describes the feeling of not knowing whether you are truly accepted, valued, or included in a group. It's not outright exclusion, but a persistent ambiguity: *Do I really fit here? Is it safe to speak honestly? Does my contribution matter?*

In schools, belonging uncertainty often shows up as self-censorship in meetings, silence in optional forums, or staff who nod politely in public but vent privately.

The Conversation Circles unintentionally amplified this uncertainty. By controlling the agenda, avoiding cultural issues, and then letting the initiative fade, leadership reinforced doubt rather than reducing it.

By contrast, the University of Cumbria's People & Culture Strategy tackles belonging uncertainty directly. Its KPIs measure whether staff feel clear about their role, receive regular feedback, would recommend the university as a place to work, and believe equality and inclusion are priorities. In doing so, it shifts belonging from an assumption to an accountable outcome.

This is the contrast between listening once and building a culture where listening lasts.

The University of Cumbria offers a very different model. The Towards 2030 People and Culture Strategy begins with clear pledges to ensure accountability, communicate proactively, equip staff for success, prioritize health and well-being, and promote equality and inclusion. But the real strength is not in the commitments alone. Each is tied to measurable KPIs, with baselines and ambitious targets that hold leaders accountable for progress. Staff clarity about their contribution to the university's success was already at 84%, with a target of 95% by 2026. Seventy percent reported receiving regular feedback from their managers, aiming for 80%. Seventy-two percent said they would recommend the university as a good place to work, with a goal of reaching 80%. Wellbeing, communication, and equality were tracked annually and openly.

This is what it looks like when listening is more than an event. When it becomes a system. Seen side by side, the difference becomes striking.

Case Study Contrast: Community Conversation Circles vs Cumbria KPIs

The Community Conversation Circles

- Sixteen sessions launched with no clear WHO, WHY, or HOW.

- Topics restricted to budgeting and facilities, culture, and safety left off the table.

- Attendance was dismal: two sessions with no one, ten with fewer than two attendees.

- No baseline, no follow-up, no reflection.

- Outcome: **staff disengagement** and reinforced mistrust.

The University of Cumbria Approach (Towards 2030, People & Culture Strategy)

- Five clear **People Pledges**: accountability, proactive communication, equipping staff, wellbeing, and inclusion.

- Each pledge is tied to **specific KPIs** with baselines and measurable targets:

    - 84% staff clarity on contribution to success → target 95%.

    - 70% staff receiving regular feedback → target 80%.

    - 72% recommending the university as a good place to work → target 80%.

    - Wellbeing, communication, and equality tracked annually with rising targets.

- Outcome: **staff voice embedded in strategy** with accountability for progress.

The Lesson

Events fade. Systems endure.

When wellness, belonging, and staff voice are anchored in strategy and measured with clarity, they shape culture over time. Without that anchor, even well-intentioned initiatives collapse into drift.

This is why strategy cannot begin with tactics. It must start with clarity. WHO we are, WHY we act, HOW we'll measure progress, and only then, WHAT we'll do.

The Bullseye Engine: WHY, HOW, WHAT

Once you've defined your **WHO** (Who we are, what we value, and what makes us unique) and your **WHERE** (the current realities of your context), you're finally ready to move into action. But even then, strategy doesn't begin with doing; it starts with clarity of purpose.

Here's how that clarity unfolds:

WHY – What Do We Believe Will Have the Greatest Impact?

This is your **Desired Impact**.

- Why are we doing this?

- What change do we want to see?

- What kind of students are we trying to develop?

- What values drive our work?

Without a strong WHY, your actions become a checklist. With it, they become intentional moves toward a better future.

"Strategy requires thinking backward from a desired future state to the choices and capabilities needed now." - Roger Martin

The WHY gives direction. It's where we take a stand on what matters, not just philosophically, but operationally.

HOW – How Will We Know It's Working?

This is your **Measurement of Success.**

- What will we measure to know we're making progress?

- What signals will show we're on the right path?

- What KPIs track our movement toward the desired impact?

HOW turns beliefs into feedback. It builds the loops we need to make timely adjustments and avoid wishful thinking.

Without the HOW, we celebrate activity, not progress. We "do" instead of improve.

WHAT – What Will We Do to Move Us Forward?

Only now does action make sense.

Your **Initiatives**, the programs, systems, professional learning, structures, and tools, are how you move toward the WHO. But now they're not guesses. They're not reactions. They're deliberate.

They are no longer the strategy; they are **in service of the strategy.**

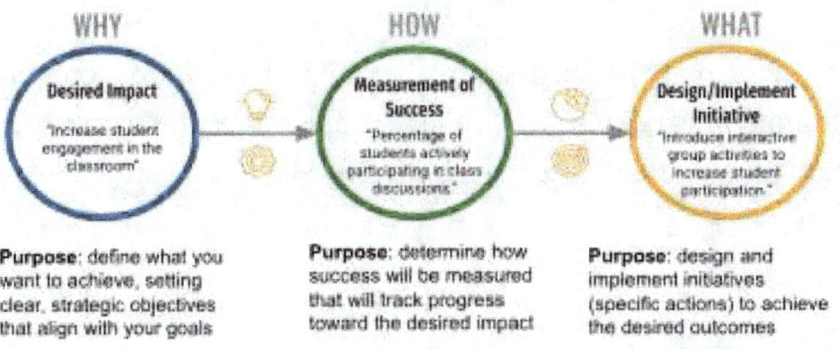

Figure: The Bullseye Engine translates clarity into action. WHY defines the desired impact, HOW establishes the measures of success, and WHAT directs the initiatives. Without this sequence, schools confuse activity with strategy; with it, every action aligns to purpose.

A Personal Reflection: Why I Would Redesign My Dissertation

When I reflect on my own work, I realize I made the same mistake I now coach others to avoid.

I wrote a dissertation on data strategy and teacher data literacy. It was thoughtful, evidence-based, and practical. But if I'm honest, it started with the **WHAT.**

We didn't have a shared **WHO**; we hadn't clearly defined what kind of learners we were trying to develop, or what type of teaching culture we needed to support them.

We hadn't established the **WHERE**, we didn't have a firm grip on our current skill levels, attitudes, or barriers around data use.

And we certainly hadn't articulated a unified **WHY** for engaging with data in the first place.

So I jumped into the implementation: creating frameworks, designing PD, and suggesting protocols. But I now see it clearly, **I was planting seeds in soil I hadn't prepared**.

And that misstep had a real consequence: the work didn't stick. It didn't take root.

The turning point came when my boss asked me to "submit a proposed list of data literacy training sessions for next year."

And I froze.

Up to that point, I'd been focused on culture: democratizing data, getting information into the hands of teachers, building dashboards, and encouraging use. But now, it was time to execute, to design professional learning that would directly shape how teachers used data to make decisions.

And I realized: I couldn't do it, not if I wanted to do it well.

Because the **WHO** hadn't been established, who were we trying to become as a faculty?

The **WHERE** wasn't clear: What was the baseline of skill, mindset, and trust around data?

The **WHY** had never been named: What did we truly believe would have the greatest impact on students in preparing them for a VUCA future?

Without those answers, anything I planned would be another WHAT without a reason, a menu of PD options detached from our values and vision.

So my response was honest:

"I can't, not if you want me to successfully help the teachers be data literate in the context of what we truly value."

And that's when I truly understood the value of strategic thinking.

We had MAP Growth data, **so much of it**. But without a clearly articulated WHY, we found ourselves constantly pulled in different directions:

"Look at this strand!"

"Here's a gap!"

"This student grew less than expected!"

"Should we switch our benchmark targets?"

It was like walking into a library with no idea what you're researching, and hoping that scanning random bookshelves will lead to insight.

We drifted.

We reacted.

We chased trends.

And then, the next year, we did it all again, reacting to a new report, a new cohort, or a new concern.

That's what happens when the **WHAT comes first**.

Data without a purpose doesn't clarify. It confuses.

And data literacy without strategic data objectives just becomes more noise.

If I were to do it again, I would begin by asking:

- **WHO are we trying to become as a school and as professionals?**

- **WHERE are we now in our practices, mindsets, and confidence with data?**

- **WHY does data matter in the journey we're on?**

- **HOW will we measure our progress toward that purpose?**

Only then would I design the **WHAT**, the initiative, the tools, the training, the expectations.

And maybe that's the most valuable thing strategic thinking gives us:

Not guaranteed outcomes, but **coherence.**

Not control, but **clarity.**

Strategic Action Is Anchored Action

Strategy without action is a hallucination. But action without strategy is chaos.

Too often in schools, we celebrate motion and visibility, the rollout, the launch, the staff meeting slideshow, rather than clarity and coherence. Activity gets mistaken for progress. Busyness becomes a badge of honor. But when initiatives aren't connected to a clearly defined identity, grounded context, and measurable purpose, they don't build momentum; they burn it.

That's exactly what happened with the Community Conversation Circles.

They didn't fail because leaders didn't care. They failed because leaders moved too fast into action. In their urgency to respond to negative data, they bypassed the strategic engine entirely. They skipped the grounding work. They didn't ask:

- **Who are we?**

- **Where are we now?**

- **Why are we doing this?**

- **How will we know if it's working?**

Instead, they defaulted to the first visible, doable solution.

They saw a WHAT, and they grabbed it.

And that's the danger of planning-driven leadership:

It's all movement, no momentum.

It's not that plans are bad; it's that plans, by themselves, don't create alignment. A plan can launch an initiative, but only a strategy can **sustain** one.

Real strategy begins at the core.

With **identity** (Who do we want to become?).

With **place** (Where are we starting from?).

With **purpose** (Why does this matter?).

And with **evidence** (How will we know we're making progress?).

Only then, and **only** then, should we move to the WHAT.

Action becomes powerful not because it's fast, but because it's aligned.

Unanchored actions not only waste time, but they also erode trust. Staff become fatigued. Initiatives come and go. Cynicism grows. And the next time leadership says, "We're listening," fewer people believe them.

Strategic action isn't louder. It's **clearer.** It connects belief to behavior. It builds momentum by design, not by hope.

Figure: Preventing drift requires anchoring action in strategy. WHO defines identity, WHERE clarifies context, WHY sets purpose, HOW measures progress, and WHAT directs initiatives. Without this sequence, schools confuse motion for momentum; with it, action becomes aligned and sustainable.

Reflection Prompt

Think about your most recent initiative.

- Did it start with a WHO, a WHERE, and a WHY?

- Or did it start with a WHAT?

- Was the HOW (success metrics, KPIs, feedback loops) clearly defined?

- Did it create **psychological safety** or **performative visibility**?

- Most importantly, **did you ask the people affected what they needed?**

If the answer is unclear, that's not failure, that's insight.

And insight is the first spark of strategy.

End of Chapter 6: Strategy in Action

"Strategy is not a slogan. It's not a checklist. It's not a plan. It's a theory of success." Chapter 6, That's Not Strategy

If you've made it this far, you've seen how strategic clarity must begin with a deliberate sense of **WHO you are becoming**, grounded in your current **WHERE**, animated by your **WHY,** measured by your **HOW**, and activated through intentional **WHATs**.

But what does this look like in a real school?

At my future school, we would build our strategy not on generic improvement goals, but on **identity-shaping choices** across six key areas: Social-Emotional Learning, Approaches to Learning, Reading, Mathematics, Staff Wellness, and Professionalism.

Each one is aligned to our Bullseye Model.

Each one names a clear identity.

Each one is measured and lived in practice.

What follows are our **Bullseye Strategy One-Pagers**, a snapshot of strategy in motion.

BULLSEYE STRATEGY ONE-PAGER, WHO WE ARE BECOMING

WHO are we becoming?

We would build a community of learners who are:

- **Empathetic, Resilient, and Grounded in Integrity**

(SEL), Students and staff who act with values, regulate emotions, and contribute positively to relationships and communities.

- **Strategic, Reflective, and Self-Directed**

(ATL), Learners who manage their own growth, adapt to challenges, and take ownership of their learning.

- **Confident, Fluent, and Reasoned Thinkers**

(Math), Problem-solvers who apply mathematical understanding with purpose, flexibility, and clarity.

- **Engaged, Proficient, and Critical Readers**

(Reading), Readers who comprehend deeply, think critically, and connect texts to real-world contexts.

- **Well, Fulfilled, and Connected Educators**

(Wellness), Staff who experience psychological safety, professional satisfaction, and a sense of belonging.

- **Professional, Accountable, and Purpose-Driven Teams**

(Professionalism), Adults who pursue growth, collaborate effectively, and uphold our shared mission with integrity.

WHERE are we now?

Most schools are in motion, strong in many areas, but in need of **strategic clarity**.

You can launch powerful initiatives, but without a shared vision of **who we're building**, efforts can become siloed, reactive, or fragmented.

WHY does it matter?

When we name the **identity** we're shaping, we create purpose-driven coherence across classrooms, departments, and leadership.

We stop chasing disconnected programs and start aligning efforts to a shared future.

HOW will we measure success?

Area	Core KPI Example
SEL	Student SEL growth & sense of belonging

ATL	Evidence of reflection & self-directed action
Math	% students meeting/exceeding growth targets
Reading	Reading proficiency and engagement levels
Wellness	Staff well-being & retention survey results
Professionalism	Participation in PLCs & goal-setting cycles

Detailed metrics for each area are tracked through strategic dashboards and reflective team processes.

WHAT will we do?

1. **Align Programs to Identity**, Every initiative supports the WHO we're building

2. **Use Data Cycles Across Divisions**, Teams track progress, and make responsive adjustments

3. **Lead with Purpose**, School leaders model strategy-in-action and hold space for reflection

4. **Invest in Capacity**, Targeted PD, and coaching align with strategic competencies

5. **Celebrate Progress**, Success is visible, shared, and connected to our strategic goals

Strategic Feedback Loop

Each quarter, leadership and learning teams reflect on evidence, adjust direction, and reaffirm alignment to our Bullseye.

SOCIAL-EMOTIONAL LEARNING (SEL)

WHO are we becoming?

Empathetic, Resilient, and Grounded in Integrity

Students who act with consistency between their values and actions, especially when no one is watching. They regulate emotions, build healthy relationships, and contribute positively to their communities.

WHERE are we now?

- SEL implementation varies widely across classrooms

- Staff are unclear which mindsets and skills matter most

- Fragmentation across programs (Positive Discipline, Character Strong, Maia Learning)

- Student well-being data suggests mixed outcomes

WHY does it matter?

Students with SEL competencies are better prepared for both learning and life. Emotional regulation, resilience, and value-driven behavior are the foundation for leadership, collaboration, and purpose.

HOW will we measure success?

KPI	Target
% of students demonstrating SEL competency growth	≥ 80%
Staff clarity on core SEL mindsets (survey)	≥ 85%
Student sense of belonging (survey index)	≥ 4.2 / 5
SEL integration in lesson/unit plans	100%

WHAT will we do?

1. Define TKS Core SEL Mindsets

2. Embed SEL into curriculum and advisory

3. Launch student-led Reflection Circles

4. Provide PD in trauma-informed and restorative practices

5. Track well-being metrics through dashboards

APPROACHES TO LEARNING (ATL)

WHO are we becoming?

Strategic, Reflective, and Self-Directed Learners

Students who take ownership of their learning, reflect meaningfully, and adapt to challenges with agency and purpose.

WHERE are we now?

- ATL skills are inconsistently taught, assessed, or reflected upon

- Students are overly reliant on teacher scaffolding

- Few systems exist to track growth in learning strategies

WHY does it matter?

In a world of rapid change, students must learn how to learn. Metacognition, planning, time management, and feedback-seeking are essential tools for lifelong success.

HOW will we measure success?

KPI	Target
% of students showing growth in ATL rubrics	≥ 80%
Teacher confidence in teaching ATL skills	≥ 85%
Quality of student reflection (rubric-rated)	≥ 3.5 / 4
ATL references in unit and lesson plans	100%

WHAT will we do?

1. Develop a K–12 ATL Skill Progression Map

2. Embed ATL instruction in every subject area

3. Launch student portfolios for goal-setting and reflection

4. Use common ATL rubrics across divisions

5. Train teachers on metacognition and coaching strategies

READING

WHO are we becoming?

Engaged, Proficient, and Critical Readers

Students who interact deeply with texts, question ideas, make connections, and use reading to make sense of their world.

WHERE are we now?

- Variability in reading levels and engagement across grades

- Limited use of formative data to guide instruction

- Gaps between reading fluency and comprehension in key transition years

WHY does it matter?

Reading is a gateway skill. Without it, access to content, critical thinking, and agency is compromised. With it, learners are empowered to lead, learn, and contribute meaningfully.

HOW will we measure success?

KPI	Target
% of students reading at or above grade level	≥ 85%
Student reading engagement survey	≥ 4.0 / 5
Frequency of guided reading/small-group work	Weekly
Reading data used in planning (teacher survey)	≥ 90%

WHAT will we do?

1. Professional learning on conferring and guided reading

2. Use MAP + formative data to drive flexible grouping

3. Launch reading engagement rubrics

4. Host Family Literacy Events

5. Audit and diversify classroom libraries

MATHEMATICS

WHO are we becoming?

Confident, Fluent, and Reasoned Thinkers

Students who apply mathematical knowledge flexibly and purposefully to real-world problems with clarity and confidence.

WHERE are we now?

- Inconsistent use of formative assessment in math

- Gaps in conceptual understanding, especially in transitions

- Widespread student math anxiety and low self-concept

WHY does it matter?

Mathematics is a language of logic, structure, and problem-solving. Fluency in math builds confidence and unlocks access to STEM pathways and real-world success.

HOW will we measure success?

KPI	Target
% of students meeting MAP growth targets	≥ 60%
Student confidence in math (survey)	≥ 4.0 / 5
Use of differentiated math groups (observed or logged)	Weekly
PLC engagement with math data	100%

WHAT will we do?

1. PD on formative practices (e.g., exit slips, number talks)

2. Use MAP data for targeted grouping

3. Host cross-grade math challenges

4. Support teachers with planning tools for differentiation

5. Develop common assessment tasks and moderation practices

STAFF WELLNESS

WHO are we becoming?

Well, Fulfilled, and Connected Educators

Staff who feel valued, supported, and energized by meaningful work, committed to growth without sacrificing well-being.

WHERE are we now?

- Wellness initiatives exist but lack cohesion and consistency

- Staff survey data reveals concerns around workload and support

- Disconnect between individual wellness needs and systemic supports

WHY does it matter?

Burned-out educators cannot support thriving learners. When staff are well, relationships deepen, teaching improves, and retention rises.

HOW will we measure success?

KPI	Target
Staff wellness index (survey)	$\geq 4.0 / 5$
Staff retention rate	$\geq 90\%$
Participation in wellness programs	$\geq 75\%$
Time use alignment with job expectations	85%+ aligned

WHAT will we do?

1. Launch divisional wellness initiatives (voice-driven)

2. Create space for connection and gratitude

3. Audit staff time and workload expectations

4. Offer targeted support: coaching, flexibility, leave policies

5. Track and reflect on wellness indicators quarterly

PROFESSIONALISM

WHO are we becoming?

Professional, Accountable, and Purpose-Driven Teams

Adults who grow continually, hold themselves and each other to high standards, and align daily work to a common mission.

WHERE are we now?

- PLCs vary in quality and consistency

- Professional growth is often compliance-driven, not purpose-driven

- Limited alignment between individual goals and strategic direction

WHY does it matter?

When professionalism is rooted in shared purpose, not just performance, it drives collaboration, deepens trust, and improves outcomes for students.

HOW will we measure success?

KPI	Target
% of staff engaging in reflective goal-setting	100%
PLC implementation effectiveness (rubric)	≥ Proficient
Participation in strategic PD	≥ 90%
Evidence of alignment in team documentation	100%

WHAT will we do?

1. Calibrate PLCs using common protocols

2. Link goal-setting to division-wide strategy

3. Offer differentiated PD paths

4. Use professional rubrics for reflection and growth

5. Showcase excellence through peer learning

These strategy one-pagers aren't final checklists.

They are living theories, designed to adapt, reflect, and evolve as we learn.

A clear strategy doesn't mean rigidity. It means we have an anchor to test against. When the evidence shows that something is not working, we can say with confidence: *No, not that thing*. When it shows alignment and impact, we can double down and say: *Yes, this is the way forward.*

That's the power of strategy. It doesn't lock us in; it frees us to make sharper choices. It separates the noise of trends from the clarity of direction.

Because strategy is not about what's fashionable.

It is about who we choose to become, and having the discipline to evolve toward that future with purpose.

Chapter 7: From Vision to Action – Collective Efficacy in Motion

John Hattie's *Visible Learning* is one of the most widely recognized research syntheses in education. Many educators can quote from it, debate it, or at least recall that familiar list of influences ranked by effect size. Class size, feedback, metacognition, and formative assessment have been circulated through countless workshops and professional learning sessions.

At the very top of that list sits one influence that often gets mentioned but rarely acted on with intention: **collective teacher efficacy.**

Hattie defines it as the shared belief among teachers that they, together, can positively impact student learning. Its effect size is larger than anything else. No single initiative, resource, or curriculum choice rivals the power of educators working in alignment, confident in their shared ability to make a difference.

Here is the challenge. Efficacy does not just happen because a staffroom believes in itself. It is not a motivational poster or a passing pep talk. It is the product of clarity and coherence. It emerges when strategy is visible, when priorities are shared, and when teachers see that their daily work connects to something bigger than their own classroom.

This is the pivot point of our journey. Up to now, we have been exploring strategy in theory. We have examined

WHO we are and WHERE we are starting from. Now, the question is execution: how do we turn clarity into collective power?

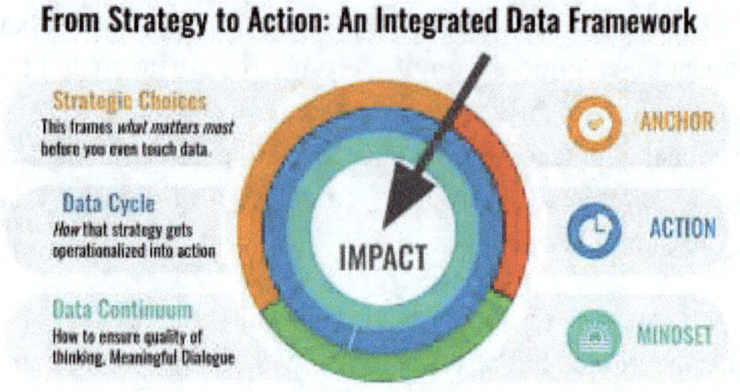

Figure: Collective efficacy is sustained when clarity, data, and mindset work together. Strategic choices provide the anchor, the data cycle drives action, and the data continuum ensures meaningful dialogue. Together, they align teachers around a shared vision and move strategy into lasting impact. (Data Cycle and Data Continuum discussed in more detail at the end of the book.)

Collective efficacy isn't something you can declare into existence. It doesn't grow out of motivational posters, staff pep talks, or optimistic emails. It emerges when clarity of values is matched by structures that reinforce commitment. And when that alignment happens, the results are unmistakable.

Strategy in Motion: The 1NU Story

I saw this dynamic clearly outside of education. Kelly and I started 1NU as a way to share our love for fitness and improving health. What began as a small idea quickly became a high-energy collective. Each session starts with ten minutes of mobility, then ten weighted stations: forty-five seconds of work, fifteen seconds to change. The circuit is repeated four times, and members can choose to swap out a round for a ten-minute block of cardio. It is demanding, but the atmosphere is electric.

At first, our structures were loose. Members could make up missed sessions whenever it suited them. It felt flexible and supportive, but in practice, it sent the wrong signal. Attendance wavered. Commitment felt optional.

The turning point came when we shifted the system. Members began paying up front for six weeks of classes. If you missed, you missed. The group moved on. It was a small adjustment, but the effect was dramatic. Attendance jumped to nearly 100%. We retained every founding member. Word spread, and new women joined each week.

Our metrics of success became clear: all the original members are still with us, new members continue to arrive, strength gains are celebrated, and the next morning's groans in the staffroom are always paired with smiles. Looking back, I can see the Bullseye model in motion. The WHO was clear: women committed to health, fitness, and encouragement. The WHERE sharpened when structures shifted from flexibility to accountability. The WHY was about more than exercise; it was about belonging, growth, and shared purpose. The HOW was the redesign of systems. Upfront payment, consistent routines, no exceptions. And the WHAT was undeniable: retention, consistency, and organic growth.

The 1NU story reminds me that values attract the right people, but structures confirm their commitment.

Back to Schools

The same truth applies in education. Collective efficacy doesn't thrive because leaders ask for it. It thrives because teachers experience clarity of purpose, structures that support them, and evidence that their work together makes a difference. When strategy is visible and reinforced through daily practice, staff don't just believe in their impact; they live it.

Carolyn and the Class of 2036

Think back to Carolyn. Her future will not be shaped by whether her teachers each did their own thing. It will be shaped by whether her teachers worked together with coherence and confidence around shared priorities.

When she enters the workforce, Carolyn will need to be adaptable, ethical, collaborative, and strategic. These traits will not come from scattered initiatives. They will come from a school that knew who it was, understood where it was, and had the courage to align around a common strategy.

Vignette: The Digital Integrity Analyst – Class of 2036

Carolyn has just landed a job as a Digital Integrity Analyst at a global platform that governs AI-curated media feeds for teens. Her role is to ensure the accuracy and emotional impact of auto-generated news summaries, memes, and video snippets. She checks AI training inputs for bias, cross-references sources, and helps design ethical algorithms that shape millions of young minds every day.

Carolyn is not only tech-savvy. She is thoughtful, strategic, and empathetic. When her team debates whether to include emotionally manipulative content for engagement, she raises the long-term consequences: the impact on mental health, on trust, and on truth itself.

She earned this role not because she memorized facts, but because she knew how to think critically and independently. She valued integrity, not just performance. She had been taught how to be a self-directed learner who questions, reflects, and makes meaning in a complex world.

This is what Richard Rumelt meant when he wrote, *"A strategy is not a goal or a vision. It is a coherent response to a significant challenge."*

Carolyn's school offered that coherent response through the Bullseye pillars:

- **Approaches to Learning (ATL):** Teachers gave her the tools to set goals, track progress, and reflect.

She learned how to direct her own learning rather than wait for instructions.

- **Social-Emotional Learning (SEL):** She practiced empathy, resilience, and integrity in every class. Emotional safety was a norm, not a novelty.

- **Reading:** Every subject treated literacy as critical. She learned to analyze bias, infer meaning, and interrogate sources.

- **Mathematics:** Math was framed as reasoning and problem-solving. Carolyn gained confidence applying logic to data, models, and ethical dilemmas.

- **Wellness:** Her teachers modeled balance and well-being. She saw that thriving adults sustain thriving students.

- **Professionalism:** Her school culture valued accountability, reflection, and growth. She witnessed adults owning their practice and aligning with a shared mission.

Collective efficacy is what turned Carolyn's story from aspiration into reality.

Book Week Reimagined

Now, let us take a different example. Wendy, the librarian, poured her heart into Book Week. She envisioned a joyful celebration of reading where students tracked their minutes, shared books, and filled the school with excitement.

But the initiative fizzled. Teachers forgot to log minutes, students lost interest, and energy evaporated. Wendy was left frustrated and alone.

The problem was not Book Week itself. It was that it began as an activity rather than a strategy. There was no shared anchor, no coherence across classrooms, and no collective efficacy.

Now imagine Book Week reimagined through the Bullseye:

- **ATL:** Students set their own reading goals and reflected on progress, making Book Week about ownership rather than compliance.

- **SEL:** Buddy reading between older and younger students built empathy and belonging, turning reading into a community experience.

- **Reading:** Teachers emphasized critical literacy, not just minutes read. Students practiced inference and bias detection alongside fluency.

- **Math:** Classes analyzed data from reading logs, graphed patterns, and applied mathematical reasoning to real-life contexts.

- **Wellness:** The initiative was designed to energize rather than burden staff. Roles were shared, and expectations realistic.

- **Professionalism:** Staff co-created the goals and measures, so ownership was collective, not individual.

Just as Denmark's Klassens Tid became a decades-long anchor for agency and belonging, Book Week could have become more than a calendar event. With strategic clarity, it could have been a building block in a culture of literacy that shaped how every student saw themselves as a reader.

The difference between the fizzled event and the transformative one is not effort. It is coherence. It is collective efficacy.

Vignette: KPIs Without Context

This problem isn't unique to classrooms. Leaders face the same trap when they try to measure success without first anchoring it in strategy.

At a data strategy conference, a director from a prominent international school asked me a question that has stayed with me: *"My board is constantly asking me for KPIs. How do I come up with them?"*

At the time, I dodged. I didn't yet have the clarity to answer. My framework then started from WHY, but I hadn't yet grasped the necessity of starting with WHO and

WHERE. Without identity and context, KPIs are just numbers. They are invented to satisfy reporting demands rather than being anchored in reality.

If I were asked that same question today, my answer would be clear:

"You can only set meaningful KPIs by first knowing WHO you are and WHERE you are. Without a baseline and an understanding of your identity, any KPI risks being arbitrary. But when you know your current reality and your desired future state, then you can set measures that actually guide improvement."

The Bullseye made this possible for me. WHO and WHERE come first. They anchor the WHY, HOW, and WHAT. A KPI like *"increase student engagement by 10%"* only makes sense if you already know the baseline and the direction you want to move.

That moment also reminded me that strategy is not innate. It is a skill. I had to learn it, and I am still learning it. And one of the greatest challenges in schools is helping leaders acknowledge their own gaps. Too often, strategy is treated as something you either have or don't. In reality, it requires humility, discipline, and continuous practice. Without that, even the best schools drift.

From Outsourcing to Ownership

This is where many schools stumble. They buy programs, rent expertise, and outsource their energy. But efficacy does not come from consultants. It comes from teachers and leaders who align their work around shared priorities.

When staff see that the school's strategy is real, not a laminated list but a living framework they helped create, efficacy rises. When they see scattershot initiatives or trend-chasing, efficacy collapses.

That is why collective efficacy is not just a statistic in Hattie's table. It is the difference between drift and direction. Between Carolyn graduating as a compliant test-taker or as a future-ready, ethical, independent thinker. Between Book Week being a forgotten event or a catalyst for lifelong literacy.

The Courage to Choose

If you want to build collective efficacy, you must choose. You cannot say yes to everything. You must define your Bullseye and align around it. That clarity is what frees teachers to believe not only in themselves but in each other.

That is not just strategy. That is strategy executed. That is how we move from vision to action.

Reflection Prompt

Think of your Carolyn, the student who will graduate into a world we can only partly imagine.

- What choices are you making now that will shape who she becomes?

- Are your initiatives aligned with a coherent strategy, or are they scattered activities that risk fading out?

- What could be your school's "Book Week" moment, and how might you reimagine it so that it builds lasting capacities rather than short-lived excitement?

Collective efficacy grows when teachers can see and believe in the through-line between their daily work and their students' future.

Chapter Wrap-Up: From Vision to Action

Strategy is not what you laminate or list. It is not the PD calendar, the consultant's slide deck, or the initiative that trends on Twitter. Strategy is a coherent response to a significant challenge, anchored in identity and sustained by collective effort.

Hattie reminds us that collective efficacy is the most powerful driver of student success. But efficacy does not emerge from good intentions. It grows when a community defines its WHO, faces its WHERE, and makes courageous choices about what matters most.

The Bullseye pillars give us those anchors: Approaches to Learning, Social-Emotional Learning, Reading, Mathematics, Wellness, and Professionalism. They are not isolated goals. They are the connective tissue that ensures every child's experience is consistent, purposeful, and future-focused.

Carolyn's journey as a Digital Integrity Analyst and the transformation of a simple initiative like Book Week into a strategic lever remind us that strategy is not abstract. It is lived. It is measured. It is collective.

When schools build strategy this way, they create the conditions where teachers believe in each other, where students grow into the future with confidence, and where vision becomes action.

Chapter 8: The School That Builds Itself

"Don't just build a school. Build the place where the future will be constructed."

In Chapter 7, we saw that collective efficacy is the engine of execution. But efficacy is not the endgame. It is the starting point for something bigger: a school that does not just carry out strategy but becomes strategy.

This chapter is about moving from anchoring to activating, from protecting coherence to building the kind of culture where clarity is lived, exported, and sustained. It is not about being known for your technology or your latest initiative. It is about being known for your clarity. Because you did not follow trends. You built the conditions where the future could be defined.

From the Outside-In to the Inside-Out

The first instinct for many schools under pressure is to look outward. They hire consultants to define the vision, adopt frameworks to fix teaching, or launch initiatives to improve culture and morale. It is an understandable reaction. When systems feel stuck, external expertise feels like relief.

But coherence cannot be imported. It must be grown. Strategic schools stop asking, "What is the best practice?" and begin asking, "What is the best version of us?" They define their own theory of impact, design systems that reflect who they are becoming next, and shape a culture rooted in context, not compliance.

Borrowed tools cannot replace built clarity.

The 20 Percent Investment

Instead of chasing consultants, schools should build them. Teachers, when invested in, become the very experts schools once thought they had to hire. With time, clarity, and trust, they can grow into the thought leaders who shape not just the future of their own classrooms but the trajectory of the entire school.

The principle is simple but powerful. Small, focused investments unlock disproportionate growth. Reclaiming even twenty percent of professional time for deep, strategic work has the potential to transform outcomes. Imagine the time spent building in-house leadership in ATL, SEL, literacy, and numeracy. Imagine structured cycles of data analysis and collaborative inquiry, faculty-led labs where teachers test and refine ideas with peers, and curriculum designed by the people who know your learners best.

The contrast is striking. Schools that fail to invest leave teachers as executors of other people's plans. Schools that invest turn teachers into architects of their own strategy.

You do not buy coherence; you build it one teacher at a time.

When people are trusted to lead, they stop waiting for direction and start shaping culture. That is when a school begins to own its strategy.

A Culture That Owns Its Strategy

You know a school owns its strategy when teachers can articulate its direction without a script, when students describe success in terms of growth and relevance, and when difficult conversations are grounded in shared language and commitments. Leaders stop chasing compliance and cultivate clarity.

Peter Drucker's line is often repeated: *"Culture eats strategy for breakfast."* For years, I nodded along, understanding it as a warning. You can have the best plan in the world, but if your culture is toxic, it will not matter. Strategy cannot survive an unhealthy workplace.

But recently, I have started to see it differently. Culture does not eat strategy for breakfast. **Culture is the breakfast**. It is the fuel, the foundation, the system that determines how strategy performs once the meeting ends and real life begins.

Schools often talk about wellness and job satisfaction as if they are the ultimate signs of health. But those things are not the goal; they are the symptoms. They are evidence of something deeper, working well or not working at all.

I had negotiated openly with a school, signed a letter of commitment, and received confirmation that they had accepted. Then, without warning, communication stopped. The school never reached out directly. The recruiter relayed that the offer was retracted, and then the school went silent.

That experience revealed something bigger than a lost opportunity. It exposed the culture behind the process. If that is how a school treats people before they even join, what would it be like inside?

I realized that my WHO, what I value most in a workplace, such as respect, transparency, and trust, was actually my WHY. It was not about wellness or job satisfaction anymore. Those are measures of culture, not replacements for it.

A healthy culture does not need to advertise its wellness program; you can feel it in how people communicate, how leaders respond, and how decisions are made. That is when I reframed my thinking.

A healthy strategy breakfast is culture. You are what you eat.

Because if culture is unhealthy, no amount of wellness initiatives will fix it. When we get culture right, wellness and job satisfaction take care of themselves.

Culture is not the soft side of strategy; it is the system that determines whether strategy thrives or fails. Schools often chase wellness as a remedy for burnout, but burnout is rarely the disease. It is the symptom of a misaligned culture. When the daily experiences of people do not reflect the values written on the walls, the result is drift. Real strategy begins when culture and behavior align, when how we treat one another becomes the clearest evidence of who we are.

So what does it look like when culture itself becomes the strategy? When belonging and clarity are not initiatives, but instincts?

Culture as Strategy: The Aspirational Bullseye

Imagine a school where culture is not something to manage but something to model.

Where clarity is lived, not laminated.

Where belonging and purpose are not programs, but proof that people matter.

This is what it means for culture to become the strategy.

WHO (Our Identity – Anchor)

We believe that culture is strategy. Our shared behaviors, relationships, and mindsets define how we teach, learn, and lead. In this school, everyone contributes to culture because everyone is accountable for how others feel when they walk through the door.

Key Values: Belonging, Trust, Psychological Safety, Shared Purpose

WHERE (Our Current Reality – Anchor)

Wellness and job satisfaction often fluctuate with workload and leadership clarity. In many schools, wellness is viewed as a program or initiative rather than a daily practice of empathy and respect. Strategic schools measure what matters most: how consistently people feel heard, valued, and connected.

Baseline Indicators: Staff satisfaction surveys, retention data, absenteeism trends, and focus-group reflections that capture authentic voice.

WHY (Desired Impact – Action)

To build a culture of collective wellbeing where every person feels psychologically safe, connected, and valued. Not because of initiatives, but because it is who we are.

Desired Impacts:

- Increased sense of belonging and shared efficacy

- Stronger engagement and lower turnover

- Daily actions that reflect integrity and purpose

HOW (Measurement of Success – Action)

We will know the culture is working when:

1. 80% of staff agree or strongly agree that "I feel valued and supported in my work."

2. More than 70% report improved well-being and job satisfaction in annual surveys.

3. Absenteeism and turnover decline by at least 15%.

4. A culture audit through 360-degree feedback confirms alignment between stated values and lived experience.

These are not metrics for compliance; they are signals of health.

WHAT (Initiatives – Action)

- **Culture Circles:** Monthly cross-division dialogues that surface challenges and celebrate growth.

- **Leadership Modeling:** Each leader participates in a reflection cycle to ensure actions match words.

- **Belonging Index:** Quarterly pulse checks that track connection, trust, and fairness.

- **Storytelling Campaign:** Shared stories of staff and students living the culture, turning values into visible action.

These are not wellness initiatives. They are systems of integrity.

Strategic Reframe

A healthy strategy breakfast is culture. You are what you eat.

When culture is nourished, wellness and job satisfaction become evidence of alignment, not outcomes of effort. Culture is the invisible architecture of every great school, the structure that holds the strategy long after the planners have gone home.

Sidebar Vignette: Culture as Compliance vs Culture as Coherence

School A: Culture as Compliance

At School A, culture lives in a handbook. Meetings begin with reminders about deadlines, protocols, and procedures. Wellness appears as a line item on the PD calendar, a checkbox beside "staff yoga" or "wellbeing week." Conversations are polite but guarded. People do what is required, not because they believe in it, but because that is the rule. When burnout rises, leaders add another initiative instead of examining the system that caused it.

School B: Culture as Coherence

At School B, culture lives in the hallways, not the handbook. Meetings begin with curiosity and connection. People feel safe enough to disagree, knowing respect is assumed. Leadership decisions are explained, not hidden. Success is celebrated collectively, and when challenges arise, the first question is "What does this say about our culture?" rather than "Who is responsible?" Wellness is not scheduled; it is sustained through trust, empathy, and shared ownership.

In the end, both schools have strategies. Only one has coherence.

Culture is not what you claim to value; it is what people experience every day. And that experience determines whether strategy survives breakfast or becomes the meal that sustains it.

Policies or programs do not power the school that builds itself; it is powered by people who live their values out loud. Culture is not the soft side of strategy. It is the side that makes every other side possible. And when culture reaches that level of coherence, something remarkable happens.

Being the School Others Learn From

When clarity becomes the norm, people stop visiting your school to see your tools. They come to know how you think. They are no longer trying to copy your PD calendar or your dashboards. They are studying your process, your discipline, and your mindset.

This is when a school moves from importing systems to exporting coherence. Teachers' voices extend beyond their classrooms. Reflection is not hidden but made public in workshops, showcases, and open meetings. Students are not passive recipients of learning but active contributors who speak with confidence to audiences inside and outside the school.

The choice is always there. You could have kept the reflection private. You could have showcased technology. Instead, you showcased thinking, shared learning, and made alignment visible.

Innovation is not what you adopt; it is what you embody.

Carolyn's Return

A decade after graduation, Carolyn walks through the gates of her old school, not as a student but as a speaker. She is now a digital integrity analyst, shaping frameworks for ethical AI governance. Yet what strikes her most is not the buildings or the technology. It is the culture.

She sees students leading learning conversations with families, portfolios open, voices confident. She watches a teacher reviewing data with a student, not to sort or label, but to reflect and adjust. She listens to a leadership team reviewing dashboards, not to police teachers, but to improve practice together. She pauses and thinks, *This is not a school that imported its future. This is a school that built it.*

There are no slogans on the walls, no buzzwords to impress visitors. What she sees is coherence made visible in the everyday choices of students, teachers, and leaders.

The future did not arrive here; it was grown here.

This is what it means for a school to build itself from the inside out.

Final Reflection Prompt

If your staff were given the time, trust, and tools to lead, what could they build?

What would happen if your school became your community's greatest investment?

Wrap-Up: Build Boldly, Strategy for a Future You Cannot Yet See

"Strategy is not about solving today's problems. It's about ensuring we have the people, the thinking, and the systems to solve tomorrow's."

This is where it all comes together. Not in a checklist. Not in a framework. But in a mindset, a way of seeing the work of education as bigger than any one program, one score, one school year.

Throughout this book, we have challenged assumptions. That strategy is a plan. It is not. It is a theory of change. That planning is progress. It is not. It is often organized avoidance. That clarity is a one-time event. It is not. It is a discipline practiced daily. That culture follows structure. It does not. Culture shapes execution, and it will eat strategy if you let it.

More than anything, we have reclaimed the idea that schools can be strategic places of design, not just responsive machines of compliance. Because education does not need more ideas, it needs better choices.

The Call to Think Future → Present

Schools are often led with a present-to-future mindset: "Here is where we are, what is the next step?" Bold strategy reverses that: "Here is the future we believe in, so what do we need to build now?"

This kind of thinking does not feel safe. It is rarely linear. It does not always earn instant approval. But it is the only kind of thinking that ensures we are not just solving today's issues, but designing for what comes next.

Strategy is how we honor the future before it arrives.

Make Fewer, Braver Choices

Great schools do not try to be all things to all people. They make bold bets on the kind of learners, leaders, and citizens they want to shape, and then they align every part of the system to that bet.

That is what strategy is: a coherent set of choices about what matters most, how we will win, and what we will need to win. It requires focus. It creates trade-offs. And yes, it invites discomfort. Without it, we do not lead. We simply respond.

That is why the strategy says: we choose this learner profile. We will measure this kind of growth. We will invest in these people. We will not be distracted by every shiny innovation with a catchy new tagline.

This is not rigidity. This is discipline with purpose.

The Real Impact

If you have read this far, you already believe that strategy in schools is not only possible, but necessary. You have seen how data can clarify, not confuse. How culture must carry strategy, not compete with it. How leadership is less about control and more about clarity and capacity.

But perhaps the biggest shift this book has invited is this: stop solving the school's problems. Start designing its future.

Because the real impact of strategy is not better spreadsheets or polished presentations, it is students who know why they are learning. It is teachers who know what they are building. It is leaders who know where they are going. And it is a community that sees its school as the most important investment it can make.

Strategy is not a reaction. It is design.

Final Thought: If Not Us, Then Who?

The work ahead will not get easier. The world will not slow down to give schools time to catch up. The stakes, ethical, human, and planetary, have never been higher.

This is why Carolyn matters. Not just the imagined Carolyn of the Class of 2036, but the real Carolyn. She was not satisfied working as a dental hygienist in a traditional clinic, so she started her own company, a mobile dental hygiene practice serving people in assisted housing, those who could not get to the dentist themselves. Carolyn knew that health begins in the mouth, and she saw the gaps in universal health care in Ontario. So she did something about it.

Her technical skills came from dental college. But the skills to build a business, design a strategy, and create a service that reached people in need, she had to teach herself. What if she had learned those attributes in school? What if her education had prepared her not only with knowledge, but with the strategic tools to design, to lead, and to build boldly? She might have launched her vision years earlier. She might have been able to help even more people, even sooner.

Carolyn's story is a reminder. Strategy is not abstract. It shapes lives. It decides whether graduates leave school merely with a profession, or with the confidence and capacity to change the world around them.

So do not just manage your school. Lead it. Design it. Build it boldly. The future is not fixed. And neither is your school. What you choose to build next will define everything that follows.

Final Chapter: That's Not Wisdom: A Glimpse into What's Next

You've reached the end of this book, but not the end of the work.

In *That's Not Strategy*, we stripped away the noise. We confronted the illusion that a colorful initiative map or a packed PD calendar equals progress. We challenged the myth that movement is momentum. And we rebuilt the foundation with one central idea: strategy is a theory of change, grounded in who we are, where we are, and what we believe will work.

But once you set a direction, a new question emerges: **How do we know if it's working?**

What Comes Next

The next book will take on that challenge: *That's Not Wisdom – Turning Data into Decisions That Actually Improve Learning.*

If strategy is the theory, then data is the test. And most schools are failing, not for lack of effort, but for lack of clarity. We are not data-poor. We are wisdom-poor.

Every school is surrounded by numbers: MAP scores, CAT4 profiles, student surveys, rubrics, portfolios, walkthroughs, SEL trackers, attendance logs, and behaviour charts. Yet when it is time to make decisions, the same questions remain: What's actually working? Where do students need the most support? Which teacher practices are moving the needle?

Access to data is not strategy. And data is not wisdom.

From Fragmented Inputs to a Data Bullseye

Just as we created a Strategic Bullseye to clarify direction, we now need a Data Bullseye to anchor the system that supports it. Schools often travel a predictable journey: from data-resistant to data-aware, to data-informed, to data-driven. But the final leap is the one that matters most: becoming data-wise.

Being data-driven means decisions are influenced by data. Being data-wise means decisions are improved by it. That final shift is the aim of *That's Not Wisdom*.

The goal is not to chase numbers, but to build wisdom.

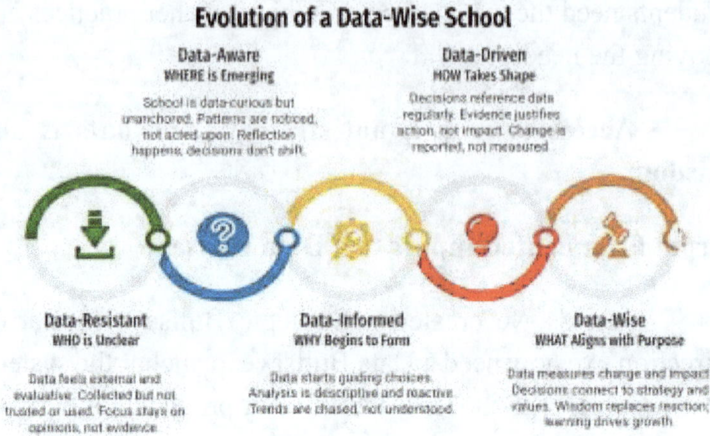

Figure: Schools evolve from resisting data to becoming data-wise. The final leap is not just being data-driven, where numbers influence decisions, but being data-wise, where decisions are improved by them. The aim is not to chase data, but to build wisdom.

The Data Continuum

Research gives us a useful frame: the Data Continuum. Data are raw pieces. Information is organized. Knowledge is interpreted. Wisdom is judgment informed by knowledge, values, and strategy.

Most schools stop at information. Some push for knowledge. Few reach wisdom. That is where impact lives. That is where data becomes not a record of the past, but a guide for the future.

The journey from data to wisdom is the journey from compliance to capacity.

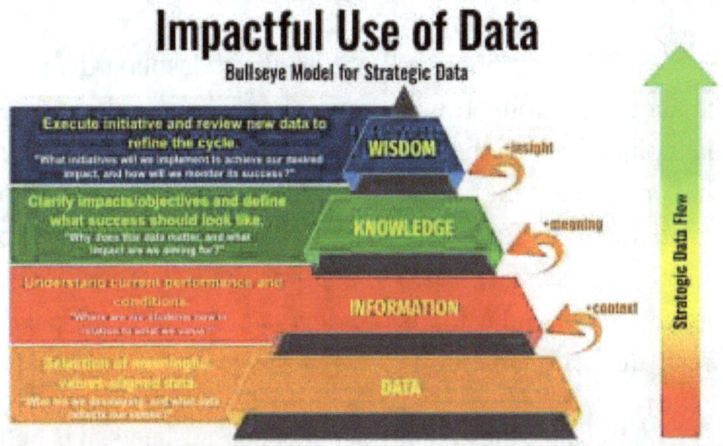

Figure: The Data Continuum shows the path from raw data to strategic wisdom. Data provides pieces, information adds context, knowledge creates meaning, and wisdom applies judgment. Most schools stop at information; impact comes when data becomes wisdom. It shapes the future, not just recording the past.

A Short Story of Too Much Data

I once sat with a leadership team staring at six dashboards projected onto one wall. There were bar graphs, heat maps, scatter plots, and trend lines. The numbers filled every inch of the screen. But when the principal finally spoke, the question was simple: "So… what do we do?"

That moment captured the truth. Data, without clarity, paralyzes. It looks impressive, but it does not move learning forward. Schools do not suffer from a lack of information. They suffer from a lack of meaning.

Wisdom begins when data turns into action.

What *That's Not Wisdom* Will Explore

This next book will not be about dashboards. It will be about decisions. It will show schools how to define clear data objectives aligned to strategy, identify relevant sources that are meaningful, and build infrastructure without mistaking tools for strategy. It will explore how to raise data fluency across staff, foster a culture where data is dialogue, not directive, and establish review cycles that keep insights fresh and actionable.

Because the goal is not better spreadsheets, it is better questions. Better decisions. And better learning.

Schools do not need more data. They need better choices.

Closing

If *That's Not Strategy* helped you define where you are going, *That's Not Wisdom* will help you prove you are getting there.

The work ahead will not get easier. The world will not slow down to give schools time to catch up. The stakes: ethical, human, and planetary, have never been higher. That is why strategy matters. That is why data must serve wisdom.

So thank you for reading. Go lead with purpose. And I will meet you in the next chapter, where strategy meets evidence and data becomes wisdom.

Wisdom is not in the numbers. It is in the choices we make with them.

References & Influences

This book was not written in isolation. It was shaped by the ideas, frameworks, challenges, and provocations of many brilliant thinkers, writers, speakers, and practitioners. Some I've learned from books and articles. Others I've listened to on podcasts, studied in courses, or had the privilege of hearing live.

Below are the voices that have directly influenced the thinking behind That's Not Strategy. Their work has sharpened my understanding of strategy, decision-making, measurement, and leadership. I'm grateful for their insights, and I encourage you to explore their work further.

Strategy & Strategic Thinking

Roger Martin

Playing to Win, The Design of Business, When More Is Not Better

Roger Martin's work on strategy as a theory of choice deeply influenced this book's distinction between planning and strategy. His focus on where to play and how to win shaped the Bullseye Strategy Model and the emphasis on coherence over activity.

Michael Porter

Famous for: Competitive Strategy, What is Strategy? (HBR, 1996)

Porter's definition of strategy as a deliberate set of choices and his warning that "you can't be all things to all people" helped reinforce the discipline and trade-offs that real strategy requires.

Rich Horwath

Strategic: The Skill to Set Direction, Create Advantage, and Achieve Executive Excellence

Horwath's work emphasizes strategic thinking as a skill, not a title. His focus on alignment, clarity, and execution helped shape how this book discusses strategic coherence within schools.

Richard Rumelt

Good Strategy Bad Strategy

Rumelt's sharp lens on bad strategy, as the failure to face a problem, challenged me to write with honesty. His idea that a plan must be a coherent response to a challenge appears throughout this book.

Measurement, Data & Impact

Stacey Barr

Practical Performance Measurement, PuMP Blueprint, and countless articles and videos

Stacey Barr's clarity on how to measure what matters and her insistence that initiatives must be anchored to measurable outcomes helped me bridge the gap between theory and action. Her frameworks appear throughout the sections on KPIs and impact.

W. Edwards Deming

Famous for: "Without data, you're just another person with an opinion."

Deming's emphasis on data-informed improvement shaped my perspective on using evidence to guide, not justify, decisions.

Jordan Morrow

Be Data Literate, Be Data Driven, and various talks and courses

Morrow's clear definitions of data literacy and his focus on turning data into action have been instrumental in framing how schools can build confidence and fluency with data.

Organizational Culture & Leadership

Peter Drucker

Famous for: "You can't manage what you can't measure" and "Culture eats strategy for breakfast"

Drucker's timeless insights on management, culture, and clarity form the backbone of many ideas in this book, particularly around measuring success and building aligned organizations.

Simon Sinek

The Infinite Game, Start With Why

Sinek's concept of infinite thinking and ethical fading appears in the chapters on drift, ambiguity, and difficult conversations. His work helped me understand why clarity of purpose is not just strategic but ethical.

Special Thanks

To the guest speakers, professors, mentors, and school leaders who challenged my thinking, asked hard questions, and reminded me that theory only matters if it changes how we serve students.